W9-BWP-580

The Secret Papers
of
Julia Templeton

THE SECRET PAPERS
OF
JULIA TEMPLETON

By Peter Cooper

Down East Books

Copyright 1985 by Peter Cooper
ISBN 0-89272-197-9
Library of Congress Catalog Card Number 85-71840

Cover design by Lynn Koski
Composition by Typeworks, Belfast, Maine
Printed in the United States of America

5   4   3   2   1

Down East Books / Camden, Maine

To Kim,
Who Inspired Cindy

CONTENTS

I WOULD LIKE TO THANK the College of St. Joseph the Provider for giving me a quiet room where, as Saturday snowfalls came down outside the window, this book took shape. I also want to express my appreciation to Dr. Michael Austin, English professor extraordinaire, for his help, comments, and encouragement.

A particular debt of gratitude is owed Keith Jennison. I was the happy recipient of the knowledge and experience this remarkable gentleman has gained from a lifetime as a writer, educator, publisher, and Vermont sage. And finally, I want to thank my typist, Mrs. Barbara Williams, and my wife, Julie, who was most helpful in the final rewrites of the book.

1 THE TOWN

It WAS THE LAST PARADE of the season in a town that loved its parades. Lots of folks sat in their cars, for most of these assemblies occurred in Vermont's chilly times; that is, spring and fall. Today was no different: the November sky was its usual lead gray. Some people also stood along the curbs. Kids were darting in and out of the parked cars. And, when the Newcastle County Courthouse clock bonged the hour, everybody started mumbling, "Parade's late," until they heard a rattle of drums up on the corner of Bass and Hard avenues.

And sure enough, here it came. In all of the parades there were certain regulars such as: Choctaw Ike, resplendent in his pure white buckskins and braid; the fat man with the pipe and wildly decorated bike; Billy Barlow in his clown suit and two-wheeled scooter; and Colonel Jim Potter, who looked just like "Black Jack" Pershing and could still wear his World War I doughboy uniform. These characters made the parades traditional.

Stepping out in back of the colors, carried by members

of the 509th Motor Transport Battalion ("You Call—We Haul") Vermont National Guard, were the city fathers and Mayor Gordon Morse. "Gordy," as he was known all over town, looked a little hunched today, probably because his doctor had him on another diet. He smiled his little rueful smile at the shivering parade watchers and hiked right along. The aldermen and town dignitaries marched sourly along in a straggly bunch. Among these was John Arnold, a youngish man who glared fiercely from beneath thick red eyebrows. He was a redheaded man whose family had lived, flourished in, and led Newcastle since 1764.

Most people, however, turned out for the bands and floats. Here came the Newcastle High Marching Band, its yellow and white uniforms adding artificial light to the gray day, and the girls' long hair falling over their trombones as they earnestly puffed away, followed by the tiniest boys with the biggest drums. Regulars who had just fallen out of Tony Pica's Grill (and saluted smartly as the colors passed by) gawked and sniggered at the bare-legged majorettes as they twirled up the street. Cars carried the fall queens—the Pumpkin Queen, Policeman's Ball Queen, and Miss Vermont—and due to the chilly day, they rode in sedans, much to the disappointment of the boys. Shriners wearing fezzes perched on little go-carts and double-ended automobiles. Kids spilled all over pioneer floats on flatbed trailers, and the crimson-and-gray-uniformed students of the Catholic school marched their banner evenly and precisely. This was Saint Francis Preparatory, a football powerhouse in the state, and a disciplined school pleasant in the thoughts of adults. Drums and trumpets called away throughout the downtown buildings until the parade ended at Founder's Plaza for some commemorative words. Mayor Morse started off the speeches before a huddled crowd.

"When, in 1764, our hardy forefathers camped along the Beaver, they could not envision the prosperous and happy city that would grow from their plans for settlement. Now old values and traditions are being tested in the caldron of . . ."

Beechmont circulated among the crowd, panhandling discreetly. He usually tried to cover his mouth with one hand while begging with the other. He knew his breath was bad, and he often dreamed of the day a wine that did not smell would be invented. Some kids danced around him hollering, "Beechmont, Beechmont, Beeeeeechmont!"

All the town called him Beechmont—he had a last name, but he rarely used it. Over the years he had become a town character, so he dropped his last name, just to be private.

He felt horrible, but that was all right—you were supposed to feel awful after drinking white port. Sighing, he received a few coins gratefully, and half-heard the speeches.

". . . so we must consecrate our efforts to the building of a better Newcastle, shining in the sun of a new day . . ." continued Morse.

I went to school with Gordy Morse, ruminated Beechmont as he shuffled at the fringes of the crowd. He always was a talker, president of our class and such, cheesum, he thought, not unkindly. In fact, Beechmont rarely thought unkindly of anybody. Even though kids teased him and most adults would rather be upwind of him, the city and Beechmont got along pretty well. He was a short man who once had a powerful build but now had a wine belly and, usually, a whitish stubble on his chin. Since 1945, when he was mustered out of the Navy, Beechmont had not held a steady job for any length of time. He was not what the social workers might call a career-oriented person. He subsisted on a veteran's pension and jobs like snow shoveling, leaf raking, and brief stints at the big commercial laundry down on China Street.

Now the bands were playing the "Washington Post March," and Beechmont began to move away from the crowd. He had collected enough for a gallon of port and he headed for the state store. After buying the wine he turned toward his little shack. But first, since he abided by the universal rule of all wine drinkers—sharing a drink—he thought he'd better go by the alley behind Tony Pica's to see if some of his friends were there. Looking into the trash-strewn alley, he saw that no one was there, so he walked on, swaying a little, down China Street to the creek. Beechmont never allowed any of his drinking friends into his shack.

On that same gray November day, Ben Weisman hung around the fringes of the parade, barely concealing a sneer as the Brownies straggled by. These hicks never saw a real parade, a real big city parade, he thought. Even that band is out of tune.

Ben and his social worker mother, Deborah, had arrived in Newcastle at the beginning of the school year. Ben was, in the eyes of his fellow students, a New Yorker, a tourist, a flatlander, and a stranger. He did little to dispel this impression, being introspective and scornful of these small-town youths. He was a sharp, darkly handsome boy of fifteen, a reader of biographies, and he buried his sensitivity in a look that warned others to stay away. But he was a good athlete and had gone out for football. Now he was thinking about a post-season party to which the entire team had been invited. He was curious (although he would never admit it) and he would go.

Parade watchers drifted away in twos and threes down streets lined with bare black trees. A cold little breeze ran around Ben as he too headed home.

He thought the worst thing about this state was that if it looked like snow, it would probably rain, and more than likely it wouldn't do anything. The horrible part of all this was that all that people talked about around here was the weather.

Home was an apartment on Lymon Street, several blocks from the business district of Newcastle. The apartment took up the entire upper floor of a square Victorian, a type abounding in this small New England town. It had two bedrooms, a living room large enough to dine in, a kitchen, and a bathroom. Ben, who was often depressed, felt more so when he entered this place. His mother, in her zeal to make it cheerful, had picked a yellow paint that had turned chalky on the old plaster walls. Over this she had hung old Olympic and bullfight posters. The rooms were clean, and the air was cold.

Ben took refuge in reading biographies—it seemed not to matter of whom—escaping into others' lives. Ben felt best when he immersed himself in his heroes' lives. Lying on his bedside table was a biography of Mahatma Gandhi. Ah, you ought to be like Mahatma Gandhi, thought Ben.

And, as was his habit, he began to envision himself as Gandhi: *He sat naked except for a thick white loincloth around his crotch on a raised, rickety wood platform in the middle of Calcutta. The sun shown bright orange on the huge crowd, which swirled and shrieked around the platform. Then he stood up and raised his brown arms and GAVE THEM THE WORD. And they all stopped swirling and yelling, and looked at him with grateful eyes, and turned and went home. He was all alone in the monstrous city square.*

"Benjamin," called a dead-even voice as the apartment's front door opened. Ben's vision of India began to disappear. The great square of Calcutta faded in his mind, and the churning crowd blurred to oblivion. "Ben, dear, are you home?" It was his mother, who always addressed him in an even voice, never loud, never angry. When Ben was at his irritating worst, his mother would still maintain a quiet that was unreal.

"Ben, dear, are you home?" She gave a tentative knock at his door. "May I come in?"

Ben sighed. "Sure."

Deborah Weisman opened the door. She was a fairly tall woman whose handsome and angular face was usually set in a serious cast, except when she smiled. "Reading again, I see. That's good, reading. Ah, books are our friends. I read a great deal as a little girl. Uh, what's the book?"

Ben's continued silence impelled her to clear her throat. "Well, supper will be ready soon. I'll see you there," she finished.

But Ben wasn't listening. He was looking out the window at a street light and he had a strange feeling that something was about to happen to him. It was a feeling he couldn't put a name to, but it was the same one he had had just before his mother told him of the impending divorce, of the move to Vermont. He remembered stifling the anger then, and the grief, choking back tears and thinking: damn them, damn them, damn them. I won't cry. I won't let her see me cry.

"Cindy." The disembodied voice floated up from below to where Cynthia O'Rourke sat, nose buried in her

notebook. "Ciiindee." The voice took on a note of command. "COME DOWN HERE."

Cynthia O'Rourke raised her head and groaned. "Yes,
Mother," she said softly to herself. Here she was, fifteen
years old, with a whole theme to write, and now her mother
wanted her to leap downstairs and wait on people in the
store. How was she going to finish? Really! she thought.

"Cynthia Susan O'Rourke, this instant!"

Cindy dragged herself away from the desk with a great
sigh and ambled downstairs.

Downstairs, her mother was shrugging herself into a
coat while three customers browsed among the shelves.
"Honey, mind the store for a few minutes while I get this
order over to Mrs. Traynor. She's sick abed, you know."

My sneaky mother, Cindy thought. Once she gets what
she wants she moves right on, no backward glances. Cindy
turned and began to play a game she played every time she
had to take care of the store. Closing her eyes she held her
breath and tried to name off every item sold in the store
before she had to breathe again: There are in O'Rourke's
Fine Foods: tissue, toilet tissue, beef jerky, jellies, jams and
doughnuts, hamburger and bologna and grade-A Maine
chicken, red wine, white wine, rose wine, old beer and new
beer, diet soda and sugar soda, ginger ale, root beer, cola,
grape, orange, cherry, raspberry, strawberry, tomatoes and
tomato juice, canned beans, spaghetti, magazines, newspapers, frozen yo—uuuuhhhhh! She let out a heavy breath.

"Miss. Oh, Miss." A man was at the counter with two
six-packs, some cigarettes, and a can of condensed milk.
Cindy whipped around the counter, rang up the order,
bingeti-bing, collected the money, said thank you, and began
to play her next-favorite store game. She called it "Strange
Order," and in it she imagined what customers did with

their orders. Like this man—he had twelve cans of beer, forty cigarettes, and a can of condensed milk. Would he sit down and smoke the cigarettes, one after another, then drink the beer, then down the milk? Or perhaps mix the milk and beer because he had an ulcer caused by all that cigarette smoking? Maybe he mixed up the cigarette tobacco with the milk and then drank the beer—aarrgh!

She thought of her family. There was her father, Michael, with his strong shoulders and arms, his black hair and pot belly. He was in Boston today negotiating with some of his suppliers. He was always telling her to read, study, and learn. He was convinced that Cindy would rise on the heights of knowledge to some exalted place in the universe.

Her mother was a mother with a capital M. She used a series of winks, grins, glowers, gestures, good and bad language, laying on of hands, and other devices to keep things running. Dad called her the Combination Fighter because you never knew what she would come up with next. And she almost always got her way.

Cindy ran down the kids. Mike, Jr., had joined the Navy after graduation. This had been disappointing to Mike, Sr., who had wanted the lad to take over the business. But young Mike, rangy, tall, and black-haired like his father, had to see the world, and Dad had to let him go. Glenda was a different story. Pretty, with the tipped nose and blond hair of a model, Glenda wanted to take over the business, but Dad had not quite accepted this idea. So Glenda bounced around from cheerleading to the drama club, did fairly well in her studies, and was held in awe by most of the high school boys. They all thought that her beauty would make her impossible to date, so she rarely went out, except with the girls. And Pete, age ten, the

Electronic Wizard, as well as the Royal-Pain-In-The-Butt. The battle lines between Pete and Cindy had been drawn about three years ago. Now they lived in kind of an armed truce, which erupted into total war from time to time. Each one kept an eye on the other. Peter, being a curious wizard, would get into Cindy's books and always leave them in a mess, or Cindy would be disturbed by an eerie wail or metallic clicking emanating from some electrical gimmick wired together by Pete.

Cindy was snapped out of her reverie by the hanging bell on the store door. Helen O'Rourke was back.

She looked at her daughter and said, "Go on back to your book, or whatever," and began restacking a display of cake mixes.

Cindy sped away upstairs and plunked herself down at the big desk in her room.

Each student in her history class had to do a project that used some town, event, or activity dealing with New England as its subject. Cindy had decided to write the whole history of Newcastle. She knew that millions of kids had tried to do this before, figuring that it would be easy. Most of them had given up and just told the story (or retold the story) of Mead's Rock.

The blurb in Newcastle's chamber of commerce brochure read:

Just west of the business district of Newcastle is the Beaver Creek. This waterway, important to the whole Beaver Valley in the eighteenth century as a power and transportation artery, is mainly used for recreational purposes today. A giant outcropping of granite situated below the railroad tracks behind Wentworth Plaza is known as Mead's Rock. Named after an early settler of Newcastle, General Llewellyn Mead, it is said to carry protection for

the town in the form of an ancient spirit. Old time Newcastle residents speak of their grandfathers who recounted
chilling tales of wild, stormy nights, and a stark white wraith
howling along the Beaver. Howling for revenge, they said.
    East of Newcastle ...

That's where most of the kids broke off usually. Well,
not Cindy. She was determined to tell the whole story,
from the first Indians who trapped around the creek right
up to Mayor Gordon Morse.

When Ben Weisman arrived at his classmate's post-
football season party, he shivered in the chill. From the
house came the sounds of disco and rock music, and
sudden bursts of laughter. Light was shining from every
window. The front door edged open and a boy stumbled
out, vomiting in the bushes as he staggered around. Finally
he disappeared around back, and Ben started for the door.
    Inside, the party paused as all parties do when a new-
comer enters. A blond kid, the host, grabbed his arm and
dragged him around.
    "This is Ben. He's new in town," he said, and the boys
glowered.
    But the girls whispered and smiled. One, wearing tight
black pants and a red bandeau, skated over (her clogs had
small plastic wheels countersunk in the soles), tapped his
nose, and said, "You're cute." Ben caught a faint scent of
alcohol on her breath as she wheeled by.
    He spurned the offer of a beer and slouched over to a
corner, a corner with books. Was there a biography here?
he wondered. He picked out a book entitled, *Mr. Lincoln's
Spy: The Story of Remember Baker.* He did not notice several of
the other boys in earnest conversation.

It seemed hours later when the blond boy tapped him on the shoulder, rousing him from the trial of the Lincoln assassins. "C'mon Ben. There's something we need your advice on, you being from the big city."

Ben's senses should have alerted him, especially as he glanced around the circle of young men struggling to keep the hostility out of their eyes. They walked into another room where Ben faintly heard some gloomy music. The light was dim, and they sat in a circle. Some of the boys sipped from beer cans.

"Ben Weisman, you're new around here," said one. Ben's depression lifted slightly, and he glanced around warily. "You're what we call a flatlander," he continued. "Anyway, we thought we'd tell you a little bit about Vermont—y'know, sorta get acquainted." A few of the boys snickered. The one who was doing the talking leaned forward. "Thought we'd let you know that around here it don't pay to act like your crap don't stink—or take things that don't belong to you," he added.

"Like girls," one of the others giggled.

"You could get hurt, y'know," the blond said.

Ben knew better than to speak up. This lousy bunch of hicks. I've watched better TV shows than this, he thought.

The blond one continued, "Around here we have ways of taking care of people who screw up."

"Yeah," slurred another in the circle. "We do 'em good."

"You gotta know, Ben, that most of the kids in this room have lived here all their lives, so have their folks, and their folks, and so on back," said his "host."

"Tell him about Saint Francis," urged another.

"Yeah," chorused the others.

"Ben, these guys have ancestors that fought Indians

with Robert Rogers in the olden times. One time they traveled on almost no food to a place called Saint Francis and killed all the Indians there, plus a whole bunch of French soldiers."

"It was horrible," said one of the beer drinkers with a Dracula laugh.

"In fact, they didn't leave a thing alive, not an Indian, or a soldier, or a baby, or a bird, or a—"

"Y'know why they did it? Because these Indians were raiding farms and killing people, and taking things that didn't belong to them!"

One of the boys leaned close to Ben and said, "An' blood is thicker than beer."

"So keep a tight ass. Don't screw up," said another.

"Don't you think it's about time for Benny to go home?" asked the host.

Ben rose slowly. His eyes were pinpoints of hate. The stupid, ignorant jerks, he thought. He felt like he was choking.

"Not that way. Not where the girls are!"

And Ben found himself outside by a spruce tree, standing alone in the damp, chill night. His heart was raging.

It was Monday morning, and Mr. Adrian Rafshoon, the high school history teacher, was asking for project topics from his tenth-grade class.

"Joseph Columbo?"

"I'm doing the history of sheep raising in Newcastle County."

"Good, Joe. Cindy O'Rourke?"

"I'm writing the whole history of Newcastle from the very beginning."

"Cindy," said Mr. Rafshoon in a condescending tone, "every class has someone who *says* they're going to do that and—"

"But I am, Mr. Rafshoon."

"They *always* wind up reciting the legend of Mead's Rock. I am getting *sick* of Mead's Rock. Anyway, I expected a more original idea from you!"

Someone sniggered.

"That's just it, Mr. Rafshoon. I really am going to do the whole thing. In fact, I'm calling it 'From Legend to Morse: A History of Newcastle.'"

The same person let out a loud guffaw.

"Quiet down. OK, Cindy, go to it. Wait. I've just had an absolutely brilliant idea. I think this is too big a project for one person, and we seem to have a gentleman in the back who is vastly amused by all this. Ben Weisman, I am assigning you to work with Cindy on this paper." There were tragic groans from both students. "Never mind the dramatics. You know your paper is due January fifteenth, and I want to see both your names on the top."

After school Cindy yelled at Ben's retreating back, "Ben Weisman, you stop running away from me!"

Ben ambled to a reluctant stop and waited until Cindy caught up, moaning inwardly: Oh man, to be stuck with this chick. Oh man, what in hell brought things to this miserable turn. The fact was, he'd been trying to figure out ways to get out of the assignment. He didn't care one bit about the rise and (hopefully) fall of Newcastle, Vermont, and having to work with this funny four-eyed dame made matters even worse.

"Now listen to me, Ben Weisman. I know what you're thinking. Never mind. We're stuck, and I am going to make this the best paper ever. Understand?" she asked.

"Uuuggh," said Ben.

"Boy, Mr. Brains from New York, is that all you can say?"

Quelling an urge to strangle this mighty mite, Ben managed to whisper, "OK, OK, Newcastle's one and only chamber of commerce."

"Listen, I'll meet you at the library at six tonight. You know where the library is, don't you? You know *what* a library is, I hope." Cindy's voice had an edge to it.

And they stood in the cold air in front of the high school glaring at each other, this solemn and handsome boy and the short girl with the big, wide glasses.

Julia Faith Templeton put down her book as she heard the late autumn wind rustle the fallen leaves outside her bedroom window. She shivered. Ah, you're getting jumpy lately, old woman! First thing you know, you'll be seeing ghosts of the dear departed, she thought. Julia shook herself and attempted to concentrate on the book. She was old and she hated to admit it. In the waning afternoon she felt fragile, and her heart seemed to be beating unnaturally. Eighty-two years, she thought, eighty-two long years in the same house. And I shall probably die here, right in this bed.

To get to Mrs. Templeton's home, you had to travel out Country Club Road about a mile until you arrived at two stone gateposts carved like Burmese temple cats. These had been a legacy from her great uncle, Samuel Coffin, who had been a merchant in the China trade during the late nineteenth century. The house perched on a hill, and was reached by a winding crushed-stone driveway bordered by Lombardy poplars. These had been planted by her grandfather, who had served in Theodore Roosevelt's administration as a special envoy to Italy. It had been in the days of "big stick" diplomacy, when America was flexing its muscles throughout the world. And Commodore Theophilus Templeton had been the very model of a merchant diplomat. A full-length portrait of him hung in the mansion's front hall. It showed a solid man, resplendent in a blue and gold uniform. His Wellington hat was trimmed in marabou, his white-gloved hand rested on the hilt of a gilded sword, and his eyes and mouth communicated a stern reminder to the world of America's might. He had embodied Victorianism—an ideal that married commercial success with blessedness, and rewarded its practitioners with power.

The house was a fine Victorian with towers and turrets, and red with white trim, all beautifully landscaped with boxwood and pachysandra. At one side was an exquisite Japanese rock garden, again reflecting the Oriental influence that can still be found dotted around New England as a legacy of its seafaring and mercantile past. This house looked great in a howling thunderstorm, with lightning lancing through gray-black clouds as rain pattered its windows.

But what of Julia herself? She had married a descendant of one of the original proprietors of Newcastle, a man who had been granted land by the governor of the New Hampshire Grants in 1764. Members of her family had been merchants and sea captains. Julia was the last of the clan to stay in Newcastle, the rest having scattered throughout the country like so many chips of New England granite.

Her husband, Henry Templeton, had died as he had lived, bitter and shouting to high heaven. He had been a mean man, stingy with the workers at Templeton Mills and cheap with the town that had nurtured his wealth. Julia had been relieved when he died, although she had worn her widow's weeds for the proper length of time.

Now Julia lived alone with a large gray cat named Old Burgoyne. She was a tall, slender woman with an open, slightly long face and pale pink skin. Her eyes were startlingly round and bright blue. Except for tonight, she was unusually vigorous for eighty-two, and normally refused all blandishments from the various senior citizens groups to join up.

Julia was a keeper of the town's history and traditions. Many politicians had made the winding trek up to her doorway to sip tea and be addressed as "young man" or "young lady" as they found out things they had never known before. It was known that all but one state governor had "visited" with Julia in the last thirty years, and the one that hadn't was a Democrat.

But now Julia sat on the edge of her bed, talking to her heart, entreating it to be slow: "Old heart, don't fail me now. The right people have not come yet, the ones who will receive my precious box." And she thought of the ancient strongbox hidden below.

Some bibulous ancestor of long ago had built an orgy room in the depths of this mansion, complete with plaster and pewter vines twisting all over the walls and cabinets, and with paintings that had brought a blush to Julia's cheeks. She had removed the paintings and burned them. Then, over the years, she had replaced them with her own handiwork—her cross-stitched samplers. She'd loved "sampling" ever since she was a little girl. It had seemed right, somehow, that those lascivious scenes should be replaced by bright, almost prim, samplers proclaiming biblical verses and tried-and-true proverbs.

It was also here, in this room of long-past gaiety, that

Julia kept the box and its possessions in a safe built into the wall. At least once every three months she made her way down the hidden winding stairway to this room, opened the door (with a key that was always around her neck), and carefully examined the contents of the box under the dim, dusty light.

When she read the old manuscripts, diaries, clippings, and jottings that crowded the box, she also glanced uneasily at the *other* box. It was a long, beautifully made black-steel container, looking like the tool box of a long-dead crafts-man. For a time after Henry's death she had not dared open it. Why, she didn't know, yet when she had reached for it she had felt a hand clutch at her heart. She had been so frightened that it had almost stopped. When she finally opened it and saw what was inside, she felt her breath go short. And when she returned the box to the safe, she had relieved it of its most precious burden.

What had been in that box reached out across the centuries. It whispered to her on late nights when the November fogs eddied around the house and she was alone with her cat and a cup of tea, growing cold in the velvet parlor.

2 THE MYSTERY

BEN WEISMAN STOOD IN FRONT of the Newcastle Free Library, watching a jet blaze a white trail through the cold November sky. As the long streamers plumed and dissipated, his mind once again chewed on the tale told him by the boys at the party. It had scared him and brought forth a sense of impending disaster. He'd never told anyone about these feelings, about how he would be in bed at night, his fists clenched close to his face, his mind on a single track of fear. And over what—a cross word from a teacher, a mine disaster in Montana, a squealing of car tires—over what? Now, he dwelled like a mole in its burrow, with the Saint Francis Massacre replaying knives, and muskets, and blood like a stuck record. He knew something was going to happen. He knew.

Cindy came bustling up, her arms filled with books. They went in, and as Cindy dropped her returned books on the counter, they asked the librarian for the key to the Wheeler Room. Cindy, who was a regular user of this room, led Ben up the stairway and unlocked the door. The room, lined with floor-to-ceiling bookcases, was filled with the history, lore, and legend of Newcastle. Here were the population figures, militia musters, merchants' bills and inventories, genealogies and lives of the founders, and all the documents and scribblings that witness mankind's struggles in tiny towns. Rooms of this sort always have a dry, papery flavor to them, and even bright days grow dim among their old wood and books.

Cindy and Ben flung themselves down at a round table. Cindy selected a light brown book from a stack that always seemed to be on the table. "Here," she whispered, "start by reading this. It will give you an idea of what Newcastle is all about."

"Hey, how come we're whispering?" he whispered back. "There's no one else here."

"It's a library," Cindy hissed. "You're supposed to whisper in a library. Now, read!"

But Ben's thoughts went again to ancient forests with Indians filing through silently, barely touching the rustling leaves, and again he experienced that creepy feeling that someone was right behind him.

"C'mon Ben, you're daydreaming. Y'know, I didn't ask for this partnership. It was Mr. Rafshoon's idea." Cindy's eyeglasses had slid down to the end of her nose.

Ben commenced reading:

> During the French and English Colonial Wars, which were known in the American colonies as the French and Indian Wars, a certain English officer by the name of Robert Rogers (at the behest of the Crown) formed the Rangers. The Rangers were attached, at various times, to the commands of Abercrombie and Howe, but had found their most fruitful service under Amherst. In this situation, they acted as scouts and commando-like raiders—a sort of

instrument of vengeance toward the Saint Francis Indians and their bloody marauding. This hardy band had trekked as far away as lands that are now known as Illinois, Michigan, Minnesota, and the Dakotas in their search for the Northwest Passage, a route they thought would lead to Cathay and the mystical Orient.

Now here was a character, thought Ben. Why haven't I read his biography?

Although Major Rogers continued to pursue his dream of finding the Northwest Passage until the day of his death, many of his original Rangers settled in the part of the New Hampshire Grants which makes up present-day Vermont. Some, as legend would have it, were thought to have received royal land grants. Although these claims have been discounted by historians, rumors and claims of royal surveyors' land parcels and outright grants persisted until well into the nineteenth century. It is possible that land was given by royal decree—it was a common form of reward for meritorious service—and that a few white settlers were there, but no record remains of their existence. In any case, land disputes occurring at this time were overshadowed by the battles fought by Ethan and Ira Allen with New York claimants to parts of Southern Vermont.

"Psst, Cindy, this Major Rogers was neat. Look at this."

Cindy sighed deeply and murmured to herself, "Why me. Why me, O powers that be?" She had been busily writing some background on the Newcastle legends, and really didn't need any interruptions, particularly on the bloody deeds of Robert Rogers.

She looked at Ben's book, and something there made her pause: "Some, as legend would have it, were thought to have received royal land grants." Cindy slipped quickly out of her chair and reached way up on one of the shelves for a slim, tattered volume with a black cover imprinted in faded gold, *Proprietorships.* She turned to the listing for Newcastle and started reading:

> Land in central Vermont, which now makes up the city of Newcastle, was in 1763 and 1764 granted to sixty-four proprietors by the governor of the New Hampshire Grants, Benning Wentworth. Many of these people never settled in Newcastle, instead selling or deeding their land to others. Among those who did settle there were Arnold and Templeton. They sectioned off the community, and it is from their plan that present-day Newcastle developed. Much of the most valuable property in the city is still in the hands of Arnold's and Templeton's descendants.
>
> There is no evidence, previous to the partnerships, that these lands were granted or settled, except for an occasional trapper or Algonquin Abenaki. Yet land boundaries were constantly in dispute in Colonial New England. In fact, it was then (as perhaps now) a main part of a lawyer's practice. Newcastle had its share of boundary and ownership quarrels. One dispute, involving land along the Beaver River, was said to have been decided in a violent fashion. This ancient tale is thought to be the basis of the "haunting" of Mead's Rock. In this legend, a ghost or specter can sometimes be seen floating aimlessly around the giant outcropping. More imaginative people claim to have heard cries or groans, as of a soul in torment and seeking revenge.

Cindy paused and thought of Ben's book. Vermont in 1763 had been under the rule of the king of England. Would the proprietors have been allowed to give away land that someone else might have already owned?

As she put the small book back into place on the shelf, a slip of paper dropped to the floor from between its pages. Picking it up and unfolding it, she saw faded, spidery writing on the faint lavender paper. What she read made the back of her neck tingle: "The proprietorships mean nothing, for there was another. Another before them. Fools."

Beechmont's home had once been a tool shack for the railroad spur that ran near Beaver Creek. Over the years, he had made it snug and warm with castoff strips of insulation, boards, flattened-out tin cans, and old Newcastle Fair posters. Very few people had been welcomed into Beechmont's home, for it reflected a different person than Newcastle was used to.

Cradling the wine he had bought after the parade, he unlocked the padlock with a key hung around his neck, and went in. His home was really one big room. Its most striking feature was floor-to-ceiling bookshelves: hundreds of books, pamphlets, magazines, and publications of all kinds filled these shelves. The books had been found or given to him, or when he had a few pennies, bought at Riford's Olde Book Emporium. Some had been thrown out by the free library and repaired by Beechmont.

The other feature of his home was an old-fashioned train-station potbellied stove that stood smack in the center of the room, its chimney running straight up through the roof. Beechmont kept it in shiny, first-class order. On the antiques market this stove would bring $1,000. He knew this, yet would never sell it.

Beechmont had stoked the stove well before he had gone out this morning, and it gave out heat aplenty; the room was cozy while outside it had become colder and a few snowflakes filled the air. Beechmont settled down at his table and uncapped the gallon jug of port. He had just taken the first warm sip of wine when there was a knock at the door.

He went instantly alert. Most people in Newcastle did not visit Beechmont at home. Most really didn't want to, and others, like the "regulars" who hung out in the alley behind Tony Pica's Grill, had long since learned to stay away. Occasionally a stranger would stumble into town, and having heard of Beechmont, would come pounding on the door. Beechmont had found that the simplest way to avoid them was to not answer.

So he was alert to this unusual knock. The first wine had begun to trickle into his veins and he felt the mounting glow. Ah well, might as well take a peek, he thought. He opened the door a sliver. It was Cindy O'Rourke. He opened the door wide.

Cindy was an exception to his no-visitors rule. Two summers ago Beechmont had fished her out of Beaver Creek when she had fallen in trying to retrieve a tangled bobber. After getting her dried off, they fell into conversation. Cindy had found Beechmont fascinating and full of odd facts, which she liked, and Beechmont had taken to this girl with the big glasses and inquisitive ways. So they had become friends. Beechmont often bought wine in Mike O'Rourke's store and never felt that *they* looked down on him.

"Hi, Beechmont."

"Good evenin', Cindy. It looks a bit like snow."

"Yes, it surely does. May I come in?"

"Why yes, you're welcome." They settled at the table. "Would you care for a glass of wine? I was jest havin' one to keep off the cold."

"No, thank you. Thanks just the same," said Cindy.

It was a ritual engaged in every time Cindy visited the

shack. Had Cindy accepted some wine, Beechmont would have (regretfully) chased her away, and that would have ended their friendship. Both knew this, and they respected each other.

"Wal, Miss Cindy O'Rourke, what brings you to visit old Beechmont on sech a cold day?" He began stuffing his old black pipe.

"It's like this: I have a class project to write, and I'm doing it on the history of Newcastle, and ... I'm kinda stuck." (She didn't mention Ben's participation, mainly because she hadn't quite accepted him yet herself.) "I've been reading about how the city was founded, and the proprietorships, and the French and Indian Wars, and Rogers's Rangers, but I'm a little mixed up. I mean, I just thought that a bunch of Colonial settlers, like Colonel Mead, happened to be farming around Beaver Creek and started Newcastle. Now I've been reading about the governor of New Hampshire *granting* the land, and yet this was in 1763, and I thought all this area was then under the rule of the king of England. Now I read that there were a whole bunch of soldiers and Rangers around, and—"

"Whoa, slow down. Yer mouth's runnin' away with yer brains. Now, try to think; what's bothering you the most?"

"I guess it has to do with those proprietorships. I mean, how could a mere governor give away land that was under the rule of the king of England?"

"Didja ever stop to think that the governor was an agent of the king?"

"OK, I can see that, but there's something else that bothers me. In the books it says there were rumors that some of these Rangers were given land as a reward for their bravery in the French and Indian War. That war was over, at least in New England, by 1760, when Canada fell. So, I guess, supposing some hero Ranger was given land before these proprietorships were granted. Supposing it was land around Newcastle. I mean, supposing—"

"Hold on, you got an awful lot of supposing goin' on here. Listen, I've read that book too. Didn't it say 'There is no evidence to—'"

"Yes. That's what it says: 'no evidence to support prior claims to the territory.'"

"Do you believe that?" asked Beechmont.

"Well, no!" answered Cindy. "But there's more. It said that there had been land disputes right up to the time of Ethan Allen, and—"

"Go on," said Beechmont.

"Well, the book mentioned the ghost of Mead's Rock. You know the legend."

Beechmont nodded.

"And when I went to put the book back, a slip of paper fell out, with writing on it."

Beechmont leaned forward, "D'ye remember what it said?"

"I—I memorized it. It said: 'The proprietorships mean nothing, for there was another. Another before them. Fools.'"

Beechmont took a sip of wine, leaned back, and began to stare hard at Cindy through a curl of pipe smoke. The girl squirmed but bravely held his stare.

Meanwhile, John Arnold, the fiery-headed lawyer, was spending the afternoon in his law office, which overlooked the business district of Newcastle.

This is when I love this town, with autumn snow cleaning the familiar buildings and depot parking lot, thought

John. For the last several days he had been thinking about the city of Newcastle, its past particularly. Something had impelled him this dark afternoon to go over and over the history of this city he and his forebears thought of as their own. He was not one to show love in word or expression, but all who knew him were aware of his devotion to the city. The Arnolds had been the first settlers, and had adopted a legacy of public service to Newcastle. At thirty-five he was a successful lawyer in the city's most prestigious law firm—Arnold, Leggett, Primrose, and Bourne.

Now he was disturbed. He had just finished talking to Julia Faith Templeton, and it had made him think of his father's death. John's father had died in a proper fashion—all pillowed up and covered by a pure white counterpane, calling the family in one by one. John remembered leaning close to his father, whose voice had sounded like paper rubbing together. The old man had muttered, "Julia . . . she . . . certain papers . . . the town . . . John . . . boy! . . . Don't let them know." And he had died with one hand upraised as if making a point to a jury.

John had not thought any more of these strange, confused words until late this afternoon. He had been idly scanning some deeds when the phone rang. It had been Julia.

"Good afternoon, Mrs. Templeton, what can I do for you?" John always called her Mrs. Templeton, out of respect.

"Never mind the formalities, young man. I used to tan your butt for stealing my apples. Julia will do, thank you very much."

"Yes, Julia."

"Now listen to me. Think back to when your father died. Do you remember anything he said?"

"I can't remember. Wait—," John's mind went back to that formal, subdued deathbed, "he said something about you and some papers. To tell the truth, I couldn't make any sense out of it."

"Oh. Perhaps it's for the best . . . he didn't tell you."

John sensed that Julia was holding something back. "Mrs.—Julia, I don't understand. Why are you calling me? What's wrong?"

"Nothing, sonny. There's nothing to tell. Just put it down to the wanderings of a crazy old lady."

"You've never been crazy a day in your life." He paused. "Wait. My father said something about the town, something about not letting 'them' know."

"It's best to let it alone, John. I'm sorry I bothered you. Let the dead stay with the dead. Goodbye."

"Julia, wait—," but she had hung up.

Julia stared at the phone, one hand pressed to her heart. She had nearly told him. Why hadn't she? Was she afraid of him? John was Maynard's son, she told herself, and the thought of Maynard Arnold brought forth a flood of memories. They had shared love and passion and tenderness when they were both young, but they never married. Julia had allied herself with Henry Templeton, owner of Newcastle's biggest mills. Maynard married the daughter of a wealthy Bennington family—a marriage of ambition.

How like the father was the son. Despite John's appearance of civic duty and good works, she knew him as a sharp and sometimes unscrupulous lawyer. Like his father, he ran his life with an absolute belief in his own rightness, and his practice as if the ends justified the means.

Lord, why did I call him? she asked herself, stroking

Burgoyne, who had curled around her slippered feet, purring.

Back in the law office, John tapped a daggerlike letter opener on the desk. His mind raced from one conjecture to another. What did she want? Those papers, do they exist? What are they, or is it just an old lady's vaporings, as she said?

He remembered the talk about her and his father. He had never been fond of her—as a matter of fact, he had hated her. She's got something, something important. He rocked slightly in his swivel chair, thinking: it wouldn't hurt to investigate. No sir, it wouldn't hurt at all.

The decison came; he had to find out what Julia knew. Picking up the phone, he dialed a number.

"Hallo, Pica's Grill."

(John covered the phone with a handkerchief.)

"Let me speak to Nick. Nick? This is the lawyer. I have a job for you."

Beechmont knocked the ashes out of his pipe and began talking in a low, soft voice. "Y'know, most folks think of the Templetons and Arnolds as the first settlers and leaders of Newcastle. 'Course what they fergit is all the other folks that have been around here just as long. Why, you take the Pica family—they been here a long time, supplyin' booze to generations of folks. Tony's pa was our biggest bootlegger, an' his father before him had a saloon. I wouldn't be surprised if the whole gang came over with Columbus and started to make hard cider out of apple squeezin's.

"An' you know Templeton Mills; there are mill workers whose daddies, and granddaddies, and *their* daddies worked there, and some of the mothers, too. Y'know Crazy Jake, the one they keep sending up to the state hospital; his folks go back to the Revolution."

Beechmont paused and sipped more wine. "Where was I? Oh, yes. You take a look at some of these books; they raise more questions than they answer. F'instance, you take George Washington, yep, the Father of Our Country. He did a lot of surveyin' all through what is now Pennsylvania and West Virginia. Did you know that in those days surveyors always plotted out a piece of land for themselves and recorded the rest for the king? Did old George do this? And, if he did, does that land belong to the people who have it now, or to all of us? After all, if George was the daddy of his country, don't that make us all his kids?"

He laughed loudly, and Cindy's eyes were as big as her glasses. Then he took a big swallow of wine and softly recited an old jump-rope rhyme:

> *Do yer ears hang low?*
> *Can you swing 'em to and fro?*
> *Can you throw 'em over yer shoulder*
> *Like a Continental Soldier?*
> *One, two, three, and out!*

"Now you might be thinkin' Cindy, that I'm a leetle teched," she shook her head vigorously, "but I'm jest sayin' you ought to look at those so-called proprietorships with a suspicious eye. There weren't so many people around to keep an eye on each other in those days, and there was an awful lot of empty land that seemed 'free' for the taking."

He paused and restoked his pipe. The light was growing dim and he turned up the lantern. There was silence interrupted only by the hiss and crackle from the fire in the railroad stove.

Cindy said, "May I go now, Beechmont? My folks will be looking for me." This also was part of their ritual, for they respected each other so much that they always asked permission to leave.

"Come again, Cindy. You are always welcome in this house."

Outside the snow-rain mixture had changed to rain, which was falling softly down, washing over the street lamps. Cindy hiked up the river bank and over the tracks. What is going on, she thought. What is going on? Her mind was a jumble of thoughts as she slip-slid her way to the store.

3 THE DEATH

CINDY O'ROURKE, HAVING ARRIVED home from Beechmont's thoroughly wet, was drying off in her room and thinking that this was a chance to get a really good grade on her history project. She could dig up some stuff no one else had seen. If there was another proprietor of Newcastle who no one had ever heard of ...

She got up quickly and dashed downstairs to the phone.

"Hello?"

"Hello, Ben. This is Cindy."

A slight pause. "Yeah?"

"Listen, I've been thinking. We have a chance to get a good grade on this history paper, 'cause I think there's something about this town no one knows," said Cindy.

"Oh," replied the voice on the other end, failing to disguise its total indifference.

"Now you wake up, Ben Weisman. I'm going to work on this—with or without you."

"Yeah."

"I'll see you in school," Cindy said. She slammed down the receiver and ran back upstairs.

Ben turned away from the telephone, thinking, What am I getting into? He didn't mind the history project so much. He was bright enough to do that. It was the girl. His mind went back to the grim little scene at the party, and the evil look of stupidity that had hung on the boys. Nevertheless, he felt a grudging admiration for Cindy and her determination to ferret out the facts behind this Vermont town. He had to admit that she was smart, and cute, too. This latter thought caused a half-smile.

His reverie was interrupted by his mother, who was explaining her tough case for the day as she served dinner.

"So I've visited his shack, place of residence, several times, and he won't let me in. And I just know the man is suffering in there. The department is ready and willing to help him. And we know he has a problem with liquor. He's probably malnourished as well. He seems nice enough; calls me Mrs. Weisman. I just don't know what to do. We must help these people."

Ben wished his mother would lighten up. His mouth ran away: "Listen, Mother, that guy's nothing but an old drunk who smells bad. Why don't you let him alone?"

"Ben Weisman, I am shocked and surprised at you! That man is a human being in need of help. Why, with a bath and clean clothes, I would think he could get a job and ... but really, Ben, to think with our background in social work ... I mean, your fa—." She stopped and reddened.

"C'mon, say it, you meant the old man. Well, he's down in New York, and we're stuck up here in the coldest state in America, where there are no Mets, Jets, Knicks, Nets, Rangers, or Yankees. I mean, you did it."

Deborah looked down at her dinner plate and said softly, "I'm sorry, Ben."

Ben felt a sudden rush of love for his mother. He spoke awkwardly, "Ah, ah . . . listen, it's OK. Excuse me." With that, he stumbled up from his chair and went to his room. Lying on the bed, he went into a fantasy: *The leader of a wagon train headed west. There he was, riding the night sentinel, watching over the mothers and kids, six-shooter at the ready— hardy, tough, and capable. Ben the Protector . . .*

As November turned into December and Christmas approached, Cindy tried to come up with an answer to her dilemma. She knew that something was not right regarding her historical findings, but where could she turn for help? If she told her father, his reaction would be: "My daughter, the brightest of the bunch. Keep at it." And then he'd tousle her hair and go back to stacking shelves.

Her mother would say, "Cynthia, don't you think they would have thought of these things before and straightened it all out? Look at all the lawyers in town. They must have things under control. Anyway, I wish you would spend more time on your arithmetic."

No, before talking to them, she'd better get the facts together. So, where was she? Taking a pencil and paper, she began to write:

1. Newcastle was founded by at least two families, who received their land in 1764 by grants from the governor of New Hampshire, who may (or may not) have been acting as an agent for the King of England, who was George III.
2. This was during the French and Indian Wars, and there was a lot of action around Newcastle, including fighting

and exploring by Rogers's Rangers. There were rumors that some of these Rangers received grants of land from the king as a reward.

3. "There is no evidence ..."
4. George Washington is the father of our country. Are we his kids?
5. Things are seldom what they seem.

Cindy sighed. Something was missing, and all she had was this feeling, what her mother called a gut reaction. Unaccountably, she thought of Ben: Boy, talk about stuck-up. But still, there was something sad about him, like he was missing something. Maybe she should call him. After all, he was on the same assignment.

Her cheeks burned a little as she thought of this dark, good-looking boy, and then it came to her—Julia Faith Templeton! Of course, why hadn't she thought of her before? Julia knew everything, and her dead husband was from one of the founding families. Cindy hoped—in fact, she was certain—that a lot of answers could be found up in the old house on the outskirts of town.

The phone rang, and finally, there was a faint click. "Hello?"

"Hello, Mrs. Templeton. My name is Cindy, Cynthia O'Rourke."

"It's Julia, and yes, Cindy, I know your father. I was wondering what took you so long to call."

Cindy felt a creepy feeling go up her back and she wondered how Julia Templeton knew she would call. "We have to do history papers in our class, and I'm doing one on the history of Newcastle. I remembered that your husband's family was a founder family, and I was wondering if—"

"Slow down, child. I knew you'd want to come up and talk. Please hurry, there's little time." The phone went dead.

"Hello. Deborah Weisman here."

"Hello, Mrs. Weisman, this is Cindy O'Rourke. May I please speak to Ben?"

"Why yes, how nice. Wait just a minute and I'll get him."

"Hullo?"

"Ben, Cindy. Listen, on our history paper, we have to go see Julia Faith Templeton."

"Who the hell is Julia Faith Templeton?"

"You don't know? I forgot, you're new here. Never mind. We've got to hurry," said Cindy. She didn't know why, but Julia had said to hurry.

"I was just lying down."

"Now lookahere, Ben Weisman, are you going to get over here, or what?"

"All right, all right. I'm on my way. Gees!"

There is a time in New England towns—usually in mid-December—when people wait for snow. It is a time of quiet. Newcastle was no exception as Cindy and Ben set out for the Templeton house. Walking through the streets in the deepening dusk, they seemed the only ones in a town of solitude.

The first few flakes were yellow and merry, like dust dancing around the street lights. The wind was at first barely noticeable as it sprinkled the snow like sugar frosting on curbs and lawns, but within half an hour it was whipping, driving it in sheets and clouds.

Cindy said, "It looks like a nor-easter." Ben didn't answer. He was thinking that Newcastle must be the weather-talk capital of the world.

Soon they had to duck and scrunch their heads into their coat collars as the wind picked up, driving the snow like sand. Ben thought this had better be worth it. He'd be dipped if he would complain in front of the pint-sized Demon Writer, though. Remember the old determination, he told himself.

The snow was piling and drifting, and Ben was in the lead. He looked back and dimly saw Cindy slip and fall. Then a power greater than his cynical self took over. He turned, reached back and grabbed Cindy's outstretched glove, and hauled her to her feet. He found himself staring directly into her face, with the big, flake-covered glasses, and long hair tangling down underneath her yellow and blue cap. He felt his heart do a great, slow roll like a stunt pilot had hold of it. He held onto her hand, and together they pulled and hauled themselves through the blasting snow until they stood on the front steps of Julia Faith Templeton's Victorian mansion.

The porch light was on. They knocked, and knocked again. No answer. Ben tried the door and it opened to his touch. They called into the gloomy hall, "Mrs. Templeton. Oh, Mrs. Templeton!"

But there was no answer as the wind howled around the house.

Cindy said, "C'mon, we'd better get in out of the snow."

Ben hesitated. "I don't know. It ain't our house."

"'Ain't' ain't in the dictionary," replied Cindy. "C'mon."

Without realizing it they had grabbed each other's hands again. Tentatively they tiptoed into the foyer.

It was dark-wood beautiful, this old house. The walls of the front hallway were made of carved light and dark cherry wood with cream panels. A full-length etched mirror stood by the old-fashioned coat rack and boot holder. Arched doorways lined either side of a long, gloomy corridor running to the rear of the house. A grandfather clock reigned over this little hall kingdom, and a broad stairway at one side led up and up.

To what? Ben asked himself. It reminded him of *Dracula:*

> *Do not be afraid, Jonathan Harker. Dr. Von Helsing is a madman; a human vampire is the superstition of peasants. But, ah, you have cut yourself! Let me look at it...*

Ben felt a sharp dig in his ribs. "Sssst, Ben the Dreamer, out to lunch again I see," said Cindy, looking up the stairway. "Oh Missus Templeton, er ..., Miz Templeton! Anyone home?"

Only the wind and snow rattled back at them.

Ben took a deep breath. "Well, we're here. W-we'd better check around, at least."

Just then they heard a faint moan from upstairs. They froze. The moan came again. Slowly, as if pulled by a magnet, they crept up the stairs. At the top, a voice, very faint, said, "In here."

A soft glow came from a half-opened door, and the two kids headed toward the light, walking like they were on ice. So intent were they to find Julia that they failed to see a figure hovering behind them. The shadow slid quietly into an upstairs room archway as they stepped through Julia's door.

"Is that you, Cynthia?" asked a cracked and tired voice. "Please say something. Announce yourself."

They crowded into the room. Julia Faith Templeton

lay pale and weak under a counterpane on her bed. With a whitened hand, looking like a statue's, she beckoned them to her side.

"Miz Templeton!" cried Cindy.

"Silence child. Come over here. I must talk to you, and there is very little time." Cindy opened her mouth to reply, but Julia snapped, "Who is that with you?"

"This is Ben Weisman, Miz Templeton. He's working on my history project with me."

"Umf, a flatlander. Well, do you love Newcastle, boy?"

Ben nearly strangled. He still had mixed feelings at this point.

"Never mind," said Julia. "Cindy, come close. I don't have much time."

"Shouldn't I call the doctor?"

"Bother the doctor. Listen to me. In the drawer of my night stand—yes, right there—is a key. Attached to the key is a tag with numbers on it. Underneath the main stairwell is a sliding door. The keyhole is covered by a piece of molding—looks like two crossed arrows. Move the arrows, unlock the panel, and you'll see stairs. Don't be afraid; there is a flashlight hanging there to light your way. At the bottom of these stairs is a door. Go in and shine the flashlight directly ahead of you. You must be quick. Don't wander." Julia hesitated as if thinking of something. "You'll see a sampler—straight ahead—it's got a border of red apples. It's the only one you want. Slide it over and you'll see a safe. The number on the key tag is the combination. Open the safe, take out the long steel box, and *leave this house.* Tell no one what you have found.

"You'll find—inside—." She began choking, and with a mighty effort went on, "the facts about Newcastle—who was here first. I tried to let them know . . ."

A recollection of the note in the library book flashed across Cindy's mind.

Julia spoke again, her voice a low rasp, "I trust you. I trust you." Her voice began to quaver, "Cindy, can you remember what I've told you? Can you repeat it?"

Cindy, scared as she was, repeated the instructions with a trembling voice.

"And please take my tomcat, Old Burgoyne. Keep him until he joins me. Please."

Ben glanced at the cat. The animal's eyes seemed to glow bright orange, and his tail stood as straight as a plume of smoke on a still day. Cindy felt tears as she petted the giant gray cat.

Julia spoke again. "I'm dying now. I have no one to see me out. Will you hold my hand so I don't have to go alone?" Cindy hesitatingly reached out her hand.

Suddenly Julia's drooping eyelids flew open. Her hands twisted, clawlike, in the bedclothes. "Child," she whispered. Cindy bent her head close to the withered lips. The voice was like a wind carrying words from far away. "Bible . . . Bible . . . the preacher. . . three . . . seven . . . three . . . please." And she died.

Cindy was crying now, but she slipped her hand into Julia's, and with the other pulled Ben closer. The wind ceased its moaning for the moment, and Old Burgoyne gazed at the tableau from his end of the counterpane.

Chief of Police Dennis Slocum stamped into the New-castle Police Department's squad room, brushing snow off his greatcoat. "It's a nor'easter, all right. Any calls?" he asked.

"Nothin' so far," said the dispatcher, going back to her needlework.

"Well, you can expect 'em—it's the night for 'em," said the chief. As if in response, the call light flashed.

"Newcastle Police Department. Please talk slower, I can't understand you. Is this some kind of joke? What do you mean Julia Templeton? Who is this speaking? Listen, kid, you can get in a lot of trouble with this kind of a call. Hello? Hello?"

"What was that all about?" asked the chief, lighting a cigar.

"Some kid tried to tell me Julia Templeton was dead. Sounded like he'd been smoking pot," said the dispatcher.

"Julia dead? The old buzzard'll outlive us all. Still, she's old." He flipped on the radio. "Car ninety-two, what's your position?" the chief asked.

The box scratched and coughed. "I'm at the corner of Grove and Ira, and it's snowin' like hell."

"Never mind the weather reports. Go to Templeton's house. We have a report of a possible ten-seventy-R there," said the chief.

"Ten-four."

The chief clicked off his transmitter, puffed on his cigar, and glanced at the dispatcher's needlepoint sampler. It read, "I Pine for You and Balsam Too."

Cindy stood by the stairway, holding Old Burgoyne and trembling. What did she mean about the Bible, and a preacher, and those numbers? Cindy asked herself.

Ben interrupted her thoughts. "That lady at the police station acted like she didn't believe me." He stood irresolutely by the stairs. "Maybe we better get out of here."

"Noooo," said Cindy, hesitating. "We promised to get the stuff from the box in that secret room. We'd better hurry—sure enough they'll send a cop to investigate."

Ben was about to argue the point, but he thought of how fervent the old lady's plea had been. "Ah, what the hell," he said.

As they crept back down the stairs, a bulky figure moved slowly to the balustrade over them, apparently watching them intently. As they groped their way along the ornately carved paneling under the stairway, the shape followed, keeping out of sight.

The wind screamed and snapped—they were in a nor'easter, sure enough.

Ben was the first to find the crossed arrows, and he pushed the piece of molding gingerly to and fro until the keyhole was revealed. Cindy inserted the odd-shaped key, turned it. A hidden spring parted the panels. A rush of cold air blew out at them, and Old Burgoyne leapt from Cindy's arms with a yowl. They peered into the gloom and saw a winding iron staircase.

Ben whispered, "It's just like 'The Pit and the Pendulum.' I really *do not* want to go down there."

Scared as she was, Cindy couldn't resist giving Ben the needle. "I really 'do not" want to go down there either, but down we go." She said this last in tones of the tomb.

Finding the flashlight inside the entrance, they started slowly down. The air seemed to get even colder and damper as they approached the bottom. Hearing a slight noise, they looked back up the stairs, only to see the panels closing ever so slowly behind them.

"Geesus! We're trapped!" hissed Ben, starting for the iron balustrade.

"Look! There's the other door—the one to the room.

Maybe we can get out through there," said Cindy. She reached for the door handle, but the door opened easily at her touch. They flashed the light inside. The beam was like a yellow butterfly, skittering over the wall ahead. What looked like picture frames flashed briefly in the light, but Cindy and Ben kept their eyes focused, as Julia had instructed, on a spot straight in front of them.

Directly ahead, just as Julia had said, was a beautifully designed, apple-bordered sampler. Gingerly they approached, and Cindy reached up and moved the sampler to one side. There was the safe. Grasping the brass knob, she turned it to the proper combination as Ben read off the numbers from the key tag. She turned the handle, and the square black door swung slowly open. Ben transferred the light to Cindy, reached in, and extracted a long box.

By this time, curiosity had wiped out fear, and they forgot all about Julia's explicit instructions to leave quickly. With Cindy holding the light, Ben crouched on the floor and opened the box.

Inside were rolls of parchment, yellowed and smelling faintly of lavender. Carefully they lifted out one of the documents, and Ben began deciphering the carefully penned words: "G—I—D—." He had spelled out just the first few letters when suddenly a tremendous crash sounded above them. Boots rang on the iron stairway, and the door to the secret room flew open.

Cindy flashed the light around to the doorway, where its beam picked up a brutal, contorted face. With an oath, the owner of the face flung Ben away from the box, grabbed it up, along with the paper Ben had dropped, and was gone, his heavy footsteps sounding fainter and fainter as he climbed the old stairway.

Then everything was silent. The light from the flash

still illuminated a narrow path where it had fallen. Ben reached a shaking hand for the light and pointed it at Cindy. Her face was nearly blanked out in the brightness as she whispered, "A-a-are you all right?"

"Yeah," Ben answered gruffly, hoping to hide the shakiness he was feeling.

The two continued to stare at each other in silence. Someone else knew about the papers. And someone else knew that *they* knew.

In the distance a police siren wailed. And they both felt the creeping fingers of fear.

The whole town turned out for Julia Faith Templeton's funeral. It was a classic New England winter's day—classic because it happens so rarely. After the storm, a blue sky and bright sun had combined with the snow to produce dazzling reflections that caused many of the mourners to put on sunglasses; a strange sight, indeed, at a winter funeral.

Mayor Gordon Morse led the solemn procession of dignitaries, including John Arnold, who appeared pre-occupied. They emerged from the big, bright Congrega-tional Church (where Julia had been a sometime suppli-cant), after the tall, deep-voiced preacher had thundered Julia's soul into heaven. This task accomplished, it re-mained only to commit her remains to a crypt, there to stay until the hard Vermont ground thawed next spring.

Both the O'Rourkes and Weismans were there, native-born and newcomer all paying tribute to the dead wife of a descendant of a Newcastle founder. Ben and Cindy stood solemnly by the crypt. They were shaking in their boots, mostly because they had not told anyone of their whereabouts on the night Julia died. They had said that they had been stuck in the library, and this was plausible, for a lot of people had been stranded in the snowstorm.

As the service droned and shivered on, Cindy allowed her eyes to wander around the crowd. There was Mayor Morse, and Mr. Arnold beside him, then Ben's mother, and Beechmont a few steps behind her. *Beechmont!* He had a real overcoat on, and it looked like a bit of necktie was peeping through above the collar. Cindy gave him a shy smile and tiny wave, and Beechmont responded with a solemn little bow. There were the fat kids who always rode red, white, and blue bikes in the parades, and there was—Cindy's eyes widened in terror—there was the man from the basement, and he was staring straight at her.

She nudged Ben, "Look, it's that guy that was in M·M·Mrs. T·T·Templeton's secret room."

Ben looked up. Sure enough, it was the man. And he looked murderous. For once Ben didn't fantasize. He pulled Cindy away from the mourners. "We're going to have to tell our parents." He tried to speak in his most grown-up voice, but it came out a squeak.

"Agreed, it's logical," said Cindy trying to put on her best lawyer air, but her voice trembled.

They looked for the man again, but he had disappeared.

4 THE CONSPIRACY

"YES, MR. O'ROURKE. This evening. I, uh, look forward to meeting your family," said Deborah Weisman, turning away from the telephone to look at her son.

She tried to look cool, wise, and understanding, all at the same time. This was difficult because visions of her son and the little O'Rourke girl, visions of infants pink-tinged and rounded, kept forcing their way into her head. Being a social worker, she pretended that they didn't exist, but she couldn't help thinking, Oh my, what has my handsome son done?

They arrived at O'Rourke's store and went around back to the outside stairway. This was Deborah's first visit to a Newcastle family, other than on official business, and she was a bit nervous. She kept glancing at her son, who was acting the soul of cool.

The door opened, and they were welcomed warmly by what Deborah thought was the handsomest family she had ever seen. Tea and cookies were pressed upon them, and introductions were made all around. Deborah felt her throat catch, and coughed to pull herself together.

The black-haired father started things off: "Mrs. Weisman."

"Please call me Deborah."

"Uh ... it looks like our Cindy and your son (Deb flushed at her thoughts) have been doing some things," he continued.

"Honey, let me explain," said the large mother. "Cindy and Ben have found out some things exploring Newcastle. They've been working on a history project together."

"What did they find?" asked Deborah, realizing that she had never thought of Newcastle as a town with history.

Mr. O'Rourke cleared his throat, "Hon, why not let Cindy tell it?"

Cindy pushed her glasses up her nose (for the tenth time since they'd been there, Ben noticed), and began. "I ... we've been working on a history project and it is, was, to cover the complete Newcastle story." She told of Ben's discovery of Ranger activity during the mid-eighteenth century, of the proprietorships, the king's grants, and her curiosity about the founding of Newcastle. She did not tell about their visit to Julia Faith Templeton's house, nor the mysterious intruder, and she especially avoided talking about her visits to Beechmont.

She was staring at Ben, who stared back in open-mouthed astonishment, and she felt a flush of shame: she had never held anything back from her parents, but she felt something holding her back, telling her, "Don't say too much, not too much."

Cindy's mother, in her characteristically blunt way said, "Listen to me. I know you've got your school work and projects and what all, but it's no excuse to be staying out late and not lettin' us know where you are. We were worried when you didn't come home in the storm. That's why we called Mrs. Weisman over."

Deborah spoke up, "Have you talked to your history teacher about this?"

Cindy and Ben looked at each other and thought of Mr. Rafshoon. Sure, he'd be interested but he'd turn it back to them for more details. If Rafshoon was anything, he was thorough.

"No . . ." said Cindy.

"I think you should let him read it—he might help."

They sat in silence until suddenly a banshee wail filled the room.

"My God, what's that?" yelled Mike O'Rourke, leaping up.

Cindy hollered, "Peter. Peter O'Rourke! Oh, Mom, he's done it again!"

Mike collared the diminutive Electronic Whiz Kid and dragged him into the room. "Say yer sorry to these folks, Peter. You made us jump a mile."

Pete mumbled something and slithered from view.

"That kid—always tinkering with that electrical stuff," shrugged Mike.

Helen adjusted herself on the sofa and returned to the subject at hand. "I got nothing against studying hard but these kids have got to keep us in mind when they go traipsin' around."

Mike chimed in, "You mind your mother, young lady. You hear?"

Ben meanwhile, had gone into an instant fantasy: *"To hell with them," swore Group Captain Reginald Smythe-Fortescue as he flipped away his cigarette. "I'll fly this mission alone."*

Soon Ben and Cindy drifted out to the hallway, munching on cookies.

Listen," Ben hissed. "How come you didn't tell about Mrs. Templeton and the secret room—and that old wino? We agreed that we would."

Cindy glared at him, "Don't you go calling Beechmont an old wino. You've got no right."

"OK, OK. But why? C'mon, out with it."

Cindy looked thoughtful. "I don't know. It was like there was someone else in the room." They stared silently at each other for a moment, then Cindy continued, "Do you want to continue with the project—I mean, the investigation?"

"The game's afoot," quoted Ben. "You don't think Sherlock Holmes would quit, do you?"

"How do you know about Sherlock Holmes?" Cindy asked.

"I read . . . I read it. I . . ." Ben stopped. His image of intellectual superiority was slipping.

They paused again, looking at each other, until Cindy broke the spell. "C'mon. We're going down to see Beechmont."

"That old wino. What does he know?"

But Cindy hushed him with a glare, and off they went as their parents' voices continued in pleasant murmurs in the living room.

Soon after Julia Templeton's funeral, John Arnold and Nick Tomasi stood in John's office, glaring at each other across a desk. Between them was a long, black, metal box.

"I told you never to come to this office. You should have left this at our usual drop." John could barely contain his fury.

"Listen, lawyer. Those kids saw me at the old lady's house. Now *that's* something to worry about." Nick was breathing heavily. He was a rough, muscular man with angry black eyebrows. His two corded, thick hands rested on the desk.

John paused and let his anger subside. Something had to be done about those kids, he thought. Hell, he didn't even know who they were. What he did know is that they knew something about this business. They had probably been with Julia before she died. He had to be alone to think. First he had to examine this box. Unfortunately, Nick had slammed the box shut so hard after grabbing it from Ben that they had to pry the latch loose together in his office.

"Nick, listen to me. I want you to leave now, but stay around. I may need you for another job."

"If you mean doin' anything to those kids, forget it. I'm not into that stuff."

John stared at him and asked himself, Was that what he had been thinking? It really all depended on what he found in this box.

"Just take off," he said, "and leave by the back. I don't want anybody to connect us."

Nick slouched out the door, muttering to himself, "High and mighty lawyer, if this town only knew what I've done for him." He began to think about the way his life was turning out.

He had been a star football player at Saint Francis Prep and had gotten an athletic scholarship to a big mid-western university, where he came within two votes of making All-America. He had wanted to be a flyer but had waited until after graduation before joining the Air Force. A career as an airline pilot had looked bright to him, but unfortunately a slight heart murmur had developed in his first year with one of the big airlines, and he washed out. Returning to Newcastle (he still maintained his single-engine pilot's license), he hung around Tony Pica's, drinking and picking up odd jobs—jobs that nobody else would do.

His mind went back to the time in his senior year when he went to the Arnolds, ashamed yet knowing they were the only ones who could help. It was supposed to be the best year of his life—a high school football star sought after by the great universities. And only a math test stood between him and the end of a triumphant football year. A lousy test, and he knew he couldn't pass it. He also knew that if he didn't pass it, he wouldn't play. The big colleges would fold up their checkbooks, turn off their "bonus" convertibles, and fade away. So he did the only thing he could do—he cheated. And he got caught.

His coach, anxious to protect his winning season, went to Newcastle's leading boosters, the Arnolds. And they were only too happy to help. After all, a football player like Nick Tomasi is a rarity in Vermont, much less their town. He had to continue to play—didn't Newcastle deserve this?

So a word to the principal, a thinly veiled warning to the hapless math teacher, and Nick's cheating became nothing but a rumor that soon disappeared in the glory of the fall football games.

In a strange way, Nick felt he owed them, even when he returned to the town years later. So he had looked up the lawyer and gone to work for him. The jobs he did for this red-headed beanpole of a lawyer soon overshadowed cheating on a school test, though, and the more he sat around Tony Pica's and the more he did for the lawyer, the more his life became entangled with John Arnold's schemes.

But there was something else that bothered him besides this lawyer's supercilious manner—something deeper, something that had to with Arnold's father and with his own family.

As soon as the door had closed behind Nick, John sat down and began to examine the black box. It was of curious handicraft, longer and narrower than the usual cash type. It was almost like an elegant tool box, elegant because it was trimmed in brass filigree resembling leaves and vines. It was a real Victorian artifact. Slowly he opened it. The lid was almost half the box, and surprisingly heavy.

Inside were rolls of paper, or more accurately, parchment. He lifted them out gingerly, fearful that they would turn to dust in his fingers. As he unrolled them on his long table, he held them down with books and paperweights. Then he began to read.

THE GIDEON TEMPLETON TESTAMENT

My name is Gideon Ivory Templeton, and having reached my seventieth birthday in this year of our Lord 1809—still in possession of my wit, a full set of teeth, and the ability to walk forth in all weather—do set down herein the true events of the founding of Newcastle.

This account reveals facts of the founding that shall forever remain hidden, for the foundation of this good town must stay marble hard and free from the rot of rumour, doubt, libel, and greed.

I was born in 1739 on a large country estate in Lancashire, England. My family was wealthy, titled, and traced its ancestry to the time of William the Conqueror, our founding ancestor, being of Norman stock. He had fought valiantly beside the brave king, and was rewarded handsomely with lands that were fertile and gladsome to the eye.

I, unfortunately, was the fifth son of an active father and bounteous mother, and, as such, was entitled to very little of the family fortune. Instead I chose the path of remittance, and journeyed to the American colonies in 1763. I arrived in Concord in the winter of 1764. This countryside reminded me of home, and I felt 'twas better here than sweating on the sun-baked plains of India playing gentleman ranker to a horse!

In Concord I had no clear purpose or direction for my life. Soon I was drinking and gambling with others of my ilk, mainly in a tavern called the Green Pine Cone. My best companions were on "remit" like myself. Their names were Daniel Southerland and Llewellyn Mead. We were all young men, bored, and full of self-pity.

Into our midst one late winter day came a young soldier of fortune who (spotting a killing at cards with us, no doubt) became ingratiating to our presence, and soon our three became four.

Our companion also brought us the news that was circulating around Concord that the Governor of the New Hampshire Grants, one Benning Wentworth, had for the past several years been granting proprietorships for lands in the West to any and all who applied. Our new companion was most conversant with this information. He went by the name of John Arnold, but once, over many cups of rum, this "English" gentleman confessed that his real name was Jean Louis Arneau, and that he had changed it to make it easier to "get my bit in the Colonies."

To tell the truth, I never liked this "John" or "Jean" even though fate would cast our lots together in mutual and damning knowledge. Suffice it to say he was a bit too clever, forever finishing one's sentences, with eyes too bright and cruel for my taste.

In any case, we made common cause with John Arnold for he knew of land so beautiful and so ready for the plow that we all envisioned great estates of our own. Could this, perhaps, sweeten the bitter memories of those lands we would never acquire in our native country?

He described the place as being one hundred miles from the Green Pine Cone, north and west. It was a small valley east of a lake, which was part of the Champlain chain and was watered by a plentiful stream called the Beaver. It's most outstanding landmark was a large rock ledge that extended out into the stream itself.

We made arrangements for acquisition of title to the land, although, it appeared, *Monsieur* Arnold did most of the arranging. So the job of first staking out our new estates went to Arnold since he was the most familiar with the territory.

Fully equipped (out of *our* purses), he sallied forth, with promises that the rest of us would follow in a few months' time.

Alas, such was not the case. Mead and Southerland, who of all of us were the most addicted to the cup, died within days of each other, shrieking lamentations in a most horrible way. So it was with much sadness that I began the journey westward alone to join up with Arnold.

My spirits soon lifted, for youth and the always change-able New England spring served to sweep away all thoughts of doom and sadness. Gusty storms and soft, warm days, along with this healthful life in God's glorious world, cleansed me of the reek of the tavern. I began to feel my health surge back, and my body took on strength, which, after all, is the proper mantle of youth.

John Arnold's directions were accurate, and after a journey of two weeks, on a sparkling May morning in 1764, I stood on a hill overlooking the most exquisite small valley I had ever seen. Tall elms and thick-trunked maples stood in majestic brotherhood with the varieties of evergreens for which this land is known. All waited for the woodsman's skill, and the soil was rich and dark and augered well for the plow. At a slight distance a gleaming stream meandered through the valley. I felt God's goodness within me.

It was then that I noticed a gray wisp of smoke eddying among the pines. Musing that it must be my partner, I decided that I would not let the thought of spending the next months (and perhaps years) with this dubious character mar the perfection of the day or my brightened spirits. Descending, I soon gained the clearing, and there was our pioneer, daubing mud in the chinks of a log cabin.

I hailed, and Arnold started, reaching for his flintlock and turning terrified eyes upon me. The fearful look did not escape me, even though when he saw 'twas I he broke into a wide grin and approached me, hand outstretched.

We greeted each other and I told him of the sad news of our compatriots. This news seemed not to disturb *Monsieur* Arnold; in fact, he treated their death as a gift that gave us more land than originally intended. I must confess that this attitude did little to dispel my misgivings regarding the man.

Nevertheless, he and I began an inspection. I was struck by the neatness of his small farm, and how solid and well built his cabin and shelters were. Land was cleared and green corn shoots were in evidence. The place looked as tidy as any farm would want to be. Of course, I complimented him on his industry.

In the days to come we saw little of each other, as I had moved to a site about three miles upriver. Life on the frontier demands unremitting toil, and I was busily clearing land and investigating the rush and turbulence of Beaver Creek. I had begun to form plans for a mill on this waterway, and I intended to harness its power to run my gears and grinders. I knew that we were but the first of a tide of settlers that would soon rush into the Vermont and Adirondack Territories now that the French were defeated and the Indian menace quelled. They would need settler's tools: axes, saws, adzes, scythes, and sickles. I saw a fine stone mill rising on the banks of the Beaver.

One day, while digging and chopping at a stubborn tree stump, my blade struck metal. Looking closer, I discovered I had found a metal box of strong construction. It had a small lock, which I broke easily. Inside were several rolled parchments. Taking them out, I unrolled them carefully.

The largest was filled with innumerable seals and fancy writing, and all protected by the great seal of England—the lion and the unicorn. Reading carefully, I saw that it was a land grant, a royal dispensation giving a certain Captain Jack Turner, as a duly appointed officer in Major Robert Rogers's famous frontier Rangers, a sizeable piece of property in the New Hampshire Grants.

I was uncomprehending at first as to how such an important document had found its way into this wilderness until I examined the other papers. Several were bills of lading from the merchantman *Lord Albemarle,* signed by Captain Turner. Another was a map.

Tracing this map and taking my bearings, I soon determined that it depicted in detail the very land upon which John Arnold and myself had settled.

The last document, and perhaps saddest of all, was the beginnings of a diary. It told of hunting expeditions and crop plantings. It showed that Captain Turner had a wife, an Abenaki woman named Kohega, who had become a converted Christian, and she had just borne him a son. This last entry was dated about a month before I had arrived on the banks of the Beaver.

By the Great Jehovah, we had usurped another man's land! Or to be more exact, *Monsieur* Arnold had taken this land. His silence had given me the impression that it all belonged to us.

I pondered what to do. I had no doubt that Arnold would kill me as quickly as he would a fly, for it appeared he had already done away with the previous tenant, perhaps by murdering him or slaughtering the entire family—who would know? My brain was in a fever of wild conjecture.

Calming myself, I decided upon a course of action.

It was our habit to meet fortnightly, sharing a supper and exchanging news. Our regular meeting was a day hence, which gave me time to find another hiding place for the box.

Upon arriving at his farm, I greeted him cordially, albeit somewhat warily. Soon we fell to talking of weather and crops and the slowly rising mill. Finally the time was ripe, and I told him of my findings.

At first he said little, but I was amazed at the transformation in his face. He had naturally pale skin, but upon hearing my account his face turned chalk white. This served to intensify his flaming red hair. His eyes glowed like coals in black sockets. I was truly afraid.

Arnold denied any knowledge of Captain Jack Turner or of ever seeing another deed to the property. He even fawned and flattered over me, calling into account our "poor" dead companions, Mead and Southerland, and how we two survivors must stick together. It was sickening, and I felt only loathing for this man.

Realizing that my life hung precariously, I informed Arnold that all the documents were hidden in a place impossible to find. Furthermore, I had sent a message by military courier to my agent in Boston as to some of the particulars of this affair, just enough to make him curious should he not hear from me regularly.

Arnold had by now fully recovered his composure, and he muttered that it all was nothing to him, and with that our meeting ended.

In the subsequent days I worked hard and saw my little

mill grow stone by stone. As the months wore on, more settlers moved in. Arnold and I, having surveyed and laid claim to a good deal of the land, parcelled it out, keeping the original titles and asking rent only when the farmer or merchant began to prosper. Meanwhile, my grinders and shapers had arrived by ox wagon, and my mill was finally able to turn out a fine quality ax blade.

Arnold proved adept at land dealings, and soon took up reading English as well as Colonial law. One day, merely by hanging a sign outside his dooryard, he became a lawyer.

So time and each day's labor managed to banish the nightmare I suffered after the discovery of the documents, and the sight of John Arnold's terrible countenance. As to the original settler's wife and child, no trace was found although there were reports of an Indian woman and child living north of our settlement. I never bothered to verify this.

Therefore these documents are to be handed down from generation to generation of the Templeton family, present and forthcoming.

To the ends of our lives we are now bound by this secret. I charge you, my descendants, to guard and protect these papers.

I have no doubt that Jean Louis Arneau, John Arnold, does not wish to pass on any account of dark deeds on his part in the acquisition of the land. But I entreat all genera-tions bearing my name to keep this knowledge secret for the protection of the town, for what I saw in the face of John Arnold that day can only be in the blood, and must be contained. I fear for our future if such a man or his heirs are given free rein in the country.

Each descendant of mine is, therefore, held respon-sible by the possession of these deeds and documents: to forever watch the tides and fortunes of the family of John Arnold; to always stand in readiness to meet with them as

I did their ancestor, and to protect our town of Newcastle from the greed and rapacity I perceived in his soul.

God grant that you do not fail.

I affirm that this is my true statement and signature, and that the only other person privy to this account is my wife, whose signature apears below.

Bethany Lucia Templeton   Gideon Ivory Templeton

The lawyer John Arnold, whose ancestor had given him his name and birthright, rummaged through the box and found the map and a meager diary.

But there was no royal decree, no deed, no grant.

Unless someone was playing a colossal fraud, the document he had just read was not only authentic, but pointed the way to another founder, another who had settled the land under royal decree.

He pressed his clenched fists to his eyes wondering, Where is it? Who has it? Those kids, perhaps those kids . . .

Outside his window, far below, fire engines wailed by as the fire horn blew its short, harsh blasts of warning.

John Arnold overestimated the extent of Ben and Cindy's knowledge of the contents of the box. The previous night they had left the family conference over O'Rourke's store and headed toward the creek to see Beechmont. Julia Faith Templeton's great gray cat, Burgoyne, had gone home with Cindy, and with regal condescension had attached himself to the O'Rourke household, which already included a pair of stray cats "adopted" by Cindy and Peter. Mrs. O'Rourke had made only a token protest about this addition to the family. Now he trotted gracefully along among the ice ruts, following the two as they made their way through the business district toward the river.

There was a light on in the little house. Cindy knocked on the door, but there was silence from within.

After a minute or two Ben said, "C'mon, he's probably sleeping it—, uh, probably asleep."

"No," said Cindy. "I think he's home. He never leaves a light on when he's away, and always when he's home a light is on. Beechmont! Oh, Beechmont! It's me, Cindy."

There was a rustle from within, and a faint voice croaked, "G'way, G'way."

"There, see. He doesn't want to see anyone," said Ben.

"No," replied Cindy, alarmed. "Something's wrong. Beechmont, please let us in."

Evidently this worked, for the door opened a crack. One tear-filled eye looked out.

"Please, Beechmont. It's me, Cindy."

The door opened wider. "C'mon in. Who's that with you?" Beechmont asked. His voice was trembling with fear.

"He's OK. He's Ben, and he's a friend. Can Burgoyne come in too? I'll explain."

"OK." The young people (and the old cat) scrambled into the riverside shack, out of the cold night.

Inside, Beechmont sat at the table, trembling as he tried to open a jug of wine. Cindy had never seen him this way—all scared, and not being wise and funny. She went over to the table, opened the wine bottle, and poured a glass for him. Then she stuffed his pipe and gave it to him. Beechmont took a large swallow and lit his pipe. Soon he stopped trembling and the color began to return to his cheeks.

"Here," he said, "I'm not minding my manners. It's cold in here." Turning to Cindy, he began their visiting ritual. "Would you like a glass of wine while I stoke up the stove?" Ben gaped, amazed at the old-timer. What nerve, he thought, trying to get this girl to drink wine.

"No, thanks, Beechmont. None for me," said Cindy.

Beechmont glanced at Ben sharply and said, "Don't understand this, do ya, boy? Well, you're in here because Cynthia vouched for you. So just set and listen."

Ben started, as if to speak, but Cindy silenced him with a short kick. She turned to Beechmont. "What's wrong? You looked like you'd seen a ghost when we came in."

"I'm awful glad to see you. I've been havin' some bad dreams. But first, what are you two doin' here, and since when did you have a cat?" Beechmont asked.

"You first," prodded Cindy.

"Wal, OK," he said, taking another swallow of port and puffing on his pipe. The room was getting warm as the railroad stove began to glow. "Before you came I was sleeping, and, I guess, dreaming. It was all mixed up. It was like I was back in the olden time. It was around here, or mebbe someplace else. It was all wilderness and there were no modern buildings. I was dressed in buckskins and had a musket and knife. We were fighting Indians. There was lots of blood and fire. I remember a priest or monk, and some kind of silver statue. Then I was by myself. It looked like right around here or over by Mead's Rock, only no buildings, just woods. Anyway, some kind of old trapper was coming at me. We fought—I knew he was going to kill me. I kept seeing an Indian woman and a baby. This feller was getting ready to run me through with his knife when you knocked and woke me up. I was scared out of my lights." Beechmont puffed furiously on his pipe.

Cindy and Ben stared open-mouthed. Finally Ben spoke for the the first time, hesitantly. "Sounds like the adventures of Rogers's Rangers. We've been reading up on this stuff. It sounds scary."

Beechment glanced at Ben with a look of relief and

gave a small smile. Then he harrumphed, "What's been going on with you two? You look like you're nervous about something, and I'm not sure I like it."

Ben and Cindy looked at each other and realized that they'd have to tell someone about their experiences. Slowly Cindy recounted the visit to Julia Faith Templeton's house, the mysterious room and wall safe, the terrifying encounter with the intruder, and finally, the family conference.

Beechmont puffed on his pipe for a while before responding.

"I think we're settin' on a stick of dynamite and it's about to go off. Someone knows somethin' they don't want the town to know, and now they know there are two kids who could spill the beans. You kids skip home—yer folks'll be worried, and when folks get worried they get suspicious. You may not see me for a little while. I don't know." Beechmont rubbed his forehead. "Anyway, take this wine jug with you. I won't be needing it for a while, at least. Now, git."

Outside, Cindy and Ben looked at each other and grinned— now they had help, and it felt good. Old Burgoyne peered and sniffed around the shack with evident approval until the three of them set out for home.

5 THE CONSPIRATORS

JOHN ARNOLD SAT, HEAD BENT, at his desk. The thought kept jumping in his brain: Newcastle was founded by my ancestor; he was French, and his real name was Jean Louis Arneau; he killed the rightful owner to get this land, and all that has transpired since that bloody day regarding Newcastle has been illegal.

He was suddenly tired—a distracted weariness stopped him from focusing on this remarkable turn of events. Then, as the light of the clear winter's morning began to stream through the tall old windows of his office, his legal training took hold. Reaching for a yellow pad, he wrote:

1. It is midwinter in the last half of the twentieth century.
2. I am a lawyer—a graduate of Harvard Law School, and a member of the Vermont Bar Association as well as the leading law firm in Newcastle.
3. My family pioneered the town of Newcastle, and my ancestor surveyed the original boundaries.
4. According to these documents, this town was founded

on a murder: the land belonged to one of Rogers's Rangers, and it was a royal grant.

5. Although I possess the authentic statement of Gideon Templeton, the royal grant is *not* here.

He thought of the two kids. How much did they know? What did Julia tell them? And who were they? He reached for the telephone.

"Hi ya, Pica's Grill."

"Nick there?"

"Yeah, hold on."

"Hello?"

"Nick, this is the lawyer. Those two kids—find out who they are and report to me at the usual place. And Nick . . ."

"Yeah?"

"Don't come to this office," said Arnold. And he hung up.

Meanwhile, on a mid-January day in the overheated school, the objects of counselor Arnold's interest were dozing in history class as Mr. Rafshoon droned on and on about the formation of the Articles of Confederation. He had already collected the history projects, including Cindy's and Ben's. Without changing his sleep-inducing tone, the history teacher asked, "Ben, what were the particular difficulties presented to the members of the Continental Congress?"

Silence permeated the room, punctured by a giggle from the only wide-awake student, a grind named Luther.

"Ben, are you with us today?"

"Huh?"

"Ah ha, a brilliant supposition. Perhaps you would care to elaborate?" said Mr. Rafshoon.

"Uh, I . . . uh, didn't hear the question."

Mr. Rafshoon's voice dripped with scorn. "Pray, my apologies, I interrupted your nap. Unforgivable. Let a poor scholar seek his answer elsewhere among this great array of brain power. Luther, please enlighten me."

After class, Cindy and Ben met outside the big red building that housed Newcastle High.

"Cripes, I am sick of winter," Ben groaned.

Cindy snapped, "Never mind that. You think Mr. Rafshoon will like the history project?"

Ben looked at Cindy and said, "You're sick of winter, too." He grinned.

"Yeah, I guess so. Ooof, it's cold," acknowledged Cindy.

"Ah, I think it'll be all right," said Ben. "We played it safe—wrote down the regular history of Newcastle."

"I guess you're right."

Both knew they were avoiding the central issue. And what made things more difficult was they really didn't know what was going on. They did know that someone was running around with a box that the late Julia Faith Templeton had said was important. Yet lately there had been a feeling of truce, as if plans were moving neither forward nor backward—or as if nothing had ever really happened. Julia Faith Templeton lay in a mausoleum under a magnificent white-marble monument depicting a sorrowing angel. The great Victorian house was shuttered, and a yellow "For Sale" sign hung out front. Most of her precious antiques and objects had been sold to antique dealers, and the town had shifted slightly, as towns will do upon the loss of a link to the past.

And Beechmont had been missing for a month.

The two kicked at icy ruts on the sidewalk in silence. Finally Ben spoke. "Listen, I've got some things to do around home."

"OK, me too. I wish we knew where Beechmont was," said Cindy.

"Yeah. Well, I'll see you tomorrow, in school."

"Sure, see ya."

And they both scuffled off, in separate directions, under the winter-gray sky.

In a nondescript green car, across from the school, a man watched the two kids as they talked. So that's them, he thought. He knew it would be easy to get identifications and report to the lawyer.

Nick Tomasi shifted in the seat of his car. He hated that lawyer; Redheaded John they used to call him in school, the same school he was now freezing his butt in front of doing the lawyer's beck and call.

He knew he was in deep. Five years of doing this man's dirty work: busting into motel rooms with a flash camera so that the lawyer could get a fat divorce settlement, shadowing a businessman, or sweet talking some records clerk to gain access to confidential files. And he hated that Arnold family.

His mind traveled back to when he was a kid. The Tomasi family had been large, boisterous, and loving. They also had owned the best restaurant in town, ideally located where the business district and residential sectors met. Growing up, Nick had known plenty of security and hard work. Everyone in town ate at Tomasi's, and the family prospered.

Nick never forgot waking up late one night and hearing hard, angry voices. He crept out of bed. Peeping over the banisters, he recognized the leading lawyer in town, Maynard Arnold, talking to his parents.

His father, who had emigrated from Sicily in 1913, still spoke in broken English. This used to make Nick ashamed, but now it made him want to kill anybody that would hurt his father.

"Hey, liss'n Meester Arnold, I been here inna Newcastle for twenny-fi' year, built restaurant up from nothin', an' now you wanna take it away?" his father asked.

"I'm sorry, Mr. Tomasi, but we expect that the new addition to Templeton Mills will bring in at least seventy-five new workers with families. And they will need housing. This area is ideal for a new highrise—already there's a parking lot. I'm sorry, but it's progress," Maynard Arnold replied.

"But . . . I don't know how to do anythin' else!" Nick's father exclaimed.

Nick's eyes filled with rageful tears. "Damn! Damn, Papa, don't beg. For Christ's sake. Don't beg," he muttered through clenched teeth.

"It's just one of those things—we need the property and the firm has decided not to renew your lease," said Arnold.

For the first time Nick's mother spoke up. "We asked you five years ago if we could buy the property and you kept putting us off. You even made promises . . ." Her voice trailed off.

"You must realize that none of that was in writing. I'm sorry, there is nothing I can do. The firm has decided," said Arnold.

"What you mean? You are the firm. You make decisions," said Nick's father.

Nick saw his father's head sink, his big work-worn hands gripped in front of him. Something exploded in Nick. He tore down the stairs, his eleven-year-old body already showing signs of the strength and suppleness that would serve him well on the football field. The adults started in surprise as the short, powerful boy hurtled into the room right at the lawyer. "Goddamn you, Protestant ba—," Nick yelled.

Quick work by Nick's father saved the lawyer from the furious assault. His mother's voice rang like a bell in the charged room. "Nick, stop it! You shame your father!"

And they all stood, frozen: the boy enfolded in his father's powerful arms, the mother straining toward them both, and the redheaded lawyer gazing impassively over his briefcase and legal papers.

So Nick (and the rest of the kids) saw the restaurant go—torn down—and a cheap-looking apartment building put up in its place. It turned out that this dwelling was never more than half-tenanted, and was soon dumped by its owners, Newcastle's leading law firm.

The Tomasi family did not fare as badly as might have been expected since Nick's father was a master chef and was able to obtain employment not too far away at a large resort restaurant in the mountains. But things weren't the same: his mother now worked, and the family, although still together, seemed not as close. Nick, thanks to his athletic ability, was able to go to college, but he had never been able to really savor life. Now he was thirty-three years old. He drank too much, had a belly, and he worked for the very man whose father had taken away the family business.

Feeling sour, he lit up a cigarette, started the car, and drove back to Pica's Grill. He needed a drink, and yet he didn't really want one.

As Ben rounded the corner on the way home, a figure stepped out and confronted him.

"Greetings, young Ben. How be ye?"

Ben stared at first, for an instant not recognizing the man in front of him. "Beechmont, is that you?"

"It be me, Ben. It sure be me."

Ben stared again. Standing in front of him was a short, powerfully built man in his fifties, wearing a fine-looking sheepskin overcoat and good L.L. Bean winter boots. Physically, the belly-bloat was gone, and Beechmont sported a neatly trimmed pure white beard. Most important, his blue eyes sparkled in the winter's twilight.

"Well, Ben, has the cat run in and stole out yer tongue?"

"No, no. Gee whiz, you look lots different."

"Well, I been over to the Veteran's Hospital. Got the booze boiled out of me and they took some weight off me. I'm feelin' pretty good. But enough about me; how's the business with, uh, our project?" Beechmont asked.

"Look, it's freezin' out here. Let's go upstairs to my place and talk," Ben suggested.

"Yer sure yer ma won't mind?" asked Beechmont.

"She won't mind. Come on."

Upstairs, Ben was amazed at himself for inviting someone into his home. Certainly he never considered asking any of the guys from school. Ever since the party where he had had that strange encounter with the boys of Newcastle, Ben had kept his distance from them. He had to fight them occasionally, particularly over his hanging out with Cindy. The fights were quiet, bloody little affairs with very little shouting, as befits a Yankee fist fight. And these fights finally stopped as the boys began to award him a grudging respect.

Beechmont spoke first: "Anythin' been happening around here while I was gone?"

"Not really. It's like nothing much has happened since Christmas. Cindy and I handed in our history project. Anyway I don't think it's going to make much difference. No one will believe us," Ben said, looking down at the floor, his usual cockiness gone.

"Mind if I smoke my pipe?" asked Beechmont.

"No, no," Ben fairly murmured.

"Sounds to me like yer givin' up too easily," Beechmont said.

Ben's head jerked up. He asked himself, Who's this old—but wait, he's not like he was.

"I've had a lot of time to think while I was at the V.A.," Beechmont continued, "an' I think there's something to all this. First, how far did you get in the history project?"

"Oh, we just wrote up everything that happened from the first settlers to right now. There's a lot of Revolutionary War and Civil War stuff, and all about the industry, and things like that," Ben answered.

"You sound real enthusiastic about it all," said Beechmont.

"Aarrgh!" Ben said.

"OK, now let's go back. Who were the first ones to be given proprietorships around Newcastle?" Beechmont asked.

Ben went to his room and dug out his copy of the history project. "The first ones were named ... let's see, John Arnold, Gideon Templeton, and Llewellyn Mead. So what does that prove? All that's in the library," he said.

"Now listen, of those, who actually came and lived in Newcastle?" Beechmont asked.

"Gideon Templeton and John Arnold," Ben responded.

"What does that prove?" Beechmont asked.

"I don't know what you're getting at," Ben said.

Beechmont went on, "Aren't the Arnolds and Templetons the founders of Newcastle?"

"Yeah," said Ben. And so what? he added to himself. He was irritated with this town again. "Yeah," Ben repeated, "there's Templeton Street, and Templeton Way, and the Templeton Factory, and Arnold Lane, and the Arnold Block—cripes!"

"For a guy that doesn't like it around here you sure have learned a lot," Beechmont observed. "So the other proprietor never did show up, is that it?"

"I guess so, but even so they named a rock after him," said Ben.

"And there it still sets, Mead's Rock, right outside my cabin door," Beechmont chuckled.

"So what does all this prove? I mean, here are two guys in the olden times that got this town started, and their names are all over the place. Y'know, I'm beginning to get sick of this whole thing. Nothing's proved. There's no record," Ben complained.

"Hold it. What about that night at Julia Faith Templeton's, the night she died? That happened, didn't it, Ben?" asked Beechmont, leaning his face close to Ben's. For an instant Ben felt a thrill of fear shoot through him as he remembered that secret cellar, and the terrible face coming at them in the gloom. He shook his head.

"Someone thinks you kids know something. And *we* have to find out what," said Beechmont.

"How come you're in on this, Beechmont? What does all this have to do with you?" Ben's tone was not harsh despite the questions.

"I don't really know. D'ya remember that dream I had down at the cabin?"

"Yeah."

"I had it again at the hospital. The same dream. And I wrote it down this time." Beechmont handed Ben a piece of paper. "Here, read it out loud."

Ben read, holding the tiny scrawls close to the lamp: "I am in a dark, deep forest and feel like I'm scared. I feel my heart pound. Then I'm being carried, and I'm above the whole scene and looking down. There is this man with a long, sharp knife hacking away at another man, who is lying on the ground. Then, I'm back being carried and moving fast. I have arms around me." Ben looked up, puzzled.

"Don't ask me, I just know this has something to do with the other dream. Anyway, I've made another list for you and Cindy."

Once again Ben read:

What We Know

1. Newcastle was founded by two men, Templeton and Arnold.
2. Julia Faith Templeton married a descendant of one of the founders. She died, leaving her cat named Old Burgoyne and some secrets concerning the town to Cynthia O'Rourke and Ben Weisman. Before these two could acquire the "secrets," the basement was robbed.
3. The person who stole the strong box saw Cindy and Ben.
4. Someone else, therefore, knows about Julia Faith Templeton's hoard.

Ben looked at Beechmont as if to ask, Where do we go from here?

Nick Tomasi and John Arnold stood shivering in the entrance alcove of an abandoned factory that once made chimney flues. It was their usual meeting place.

Nick was speaking. "The boy's name is Ben Weisman. He lives with his mother in an upstairs apartment at 17 Lymon Street. They are originally from New York City. The mother—her name is Deborah—is a social worker and works for the state. The girl's name is Cynthia O'Rourke. They call her Cindy. Her father and mother, Michael and Helen, run O'Rourke's Fine Foods on Clement Avenue. They've lived in Newcastle a long time. They were born here."

After receiving this report, John stood silently in the late afternoon cold, his thoughts in a jumble. Finally Nick spoke again: "Anything else you want done, Mr. Arnold?"

John's thoughts came back to the present and he asked, "Nick, you really don't like me very much, do you?"

"Listen, Mr. Arnold, don't ask, just don't ask. I work for you. I don't have to like you."

John took this as some kind of expression of loyalty. "Nick, somewhere in that house is a certain document— it'll be covered with fancy writing and old wax seals. It's very old. I want you to go back there and get it. I don't care how you do it, just get it and bring it back to me. Do you understand?"

"Yeah, yeah," Nick said, feeling his stomach tighten, still sour from his bitterness and the booze of the previous night. He turned away abruptly and strode off.

John stood in the cold, gathering dark, gazing abstractedly after Nick's retreating figure and thinking about the future. He was the only living descendant of a founder. His duty was clear—nothing must change the status, nothing must threaten the town! Nothing must undermine his family's prestige or cast doubt on the legitimacy of their extensive property holdings in Newcastle.

Overhead, a jet going from Burlington to Boston whistled its headlong way, leaving bright orange contrails in the chilly, deep-blue of an evening sky.

By the middle of February, Attorney John Arnold of Newcastle's most prestigious law firm had made several telephone calls. These calls set in motion a series of events.

First, a very neat, very well-dressed young man approached Michael O'Rourke's Fine Foods with a proposition. It seemed that a certain party was very much interested in purchasing the store as a retirement investment and occupation. Besides a tidy sum for the store, this party offered to throw in a similar operation in Lee, Massachusetts, in the heart of the Berkshires. It was described as a place of bounding business because of all the tourist trade, allowing the fortunate owner to go to Florida for three months of the year. This deal looked so attractive that Michael politely kicked the young man out of the store: first, because he couldn't believe it; and second, because he didn't want to disrupt the family.

Next, Deborah Weisman, MSW, was called into the office of her supervisor at the dark brick building that housed the state government offices in Newcastle. Her superior was a precise gentleman with a square mustache who tented his fingers when he spoke. "Deb, your work has been under observation and we are well pleased. In fact, the powers that be have also been checking your record and they are also well pleased." He paused to clear his throat. "There is a position open in Waterbury, a supervisory position, and we feel you are the best one for the job."

"Thank you, Mr. Dadier . . . uh, Carl. I don't know. You see, I've had a fairly difficult time getting Ben—he's my son—to adjust to living in Vermont, in Newcastle. Now he seems to be adapting well. He's met a new friend, a girl, and he's been involved in a town history project. I just don't know about moving again," said Deborah.

"Of course. Think it over, but don't take too long. This is a peach of a job—I wouldn't pass it up," said Mr. Dadier, his eyes flickering at her. The bureaucratic threat was obvious.

When John heard of the refusals (for indeed Deborah had decided to stay in Newcastle), he sat in his deep, leather lawyer's chair and gazed out at the frozen, snow-strewn city. It would soon be spring—those few days (between the wet snow, sudden freezes, and the rain and mud) of soft green that make this land so precious, so beautiful. He thought back to the documents, those ancient, damning proofs that his ancestor was a murderer, that the town was founded on violence, that there might be descendants of this Captain Jack Turner and his Indian wife. He struck the desk hard and thought: It's mine—this town is *mine*. And at once he felt a coldness, a clearness of purpose.

Reaching for the phone, he dialed Pica's Grill and asked for Nick. He had made his decision.

Old Burgoyne, Julia Faith Templeton's great gray tomcat with the golden eyes, had adopted Ben and Cindy. He trotted and prowled around wherever they went, but, reflecting his last mistress's fierce independence, he relied on his own devices for food and shelter. Cindy politely did not question Burgoyne's nighttime peregrinations, and the cat was equally courtly, never bringing back presents of belly-slashed mice or birds.

At this point he was dozing by Beechmont's warm railroad stove while the three adventurers conspired around the table.

Ben was scoffing at the other two: "What actually do we know—a couple of dreams of Beechmont's, some stories in old library books, and nothin' else."

"What about Miz Templeton's secret cellar? And that guy? And we saw him again at the funeral," said Cindy, glaring at Ben.

"He could have been after money. Everybody knows old people hoard dough," said Ben. He stopped and looked at Beechmont, his cheeks reddening with embarrassment. "Sorry."

But this worthy had been puffing his pipe, and only half listening to their squabbling. Finally he put down his pipe and said, "There's only one thing for it. We got to get back into Julia's house. I knew Julia, an' she wasn't the type to put all her eggs in one basket. Sure'n shootin', there's something else in that house that points the way."

Ben and Cindy immediately stopped quarreling, seized with the spirit of adventure. Old Burgoyne's head went up in yellow-eyed alert.

"But," warned Beechmont, "it ain't exactly legal, our messing around Julia's old house."

"Yeah," the kids breathed. Old Burgoyne bared his tiny fangs, and the three looked at one another in the dim light.

Beechmont said, "Mebbe she gave you a clue—some word or something when she was dyin'."

Cindy sat, cudgeling her brains, and said, "We went into the house. It was snowing. We went upstairs and there was Miz Templeton. She told us about the cellar and the key. She kept talking about there being so little time left, and then her voice got all weak and funny. I had to lean my head down to hear. It sounded like she was talking about the Bible, something about a preacher, and then a couple of numbers . . . uh, three and seven. I don't know, Beechmont. There doesn't seem to be much. All I can think of is that scary guy in the basement."

Just then, Ben the Suspicious spoke up. "Let's do it, let's go to the house."

They looked at him and nodded agreement.

Nick Tomasi stood behind a tree and shivered in the early March night as he watched the three figures emerge from the riverside shack. Now what are they up to? he asked himself, and belched, feeling his stomach doing the Dance of the Pitchforks. Those kids had the wino with them. That was going to make his job twice as nasty. He cursed the lawyer and shifted his grip on the heavy steel pry-bar. Now it would have to be three instead of two.

He shivered again and looked up. The sky was a boiling gray, and the air was breezy and smelled wet. The three figures headed north, and he followed. He might as well get this over with.

The rain had started by the time the three intrepid souls arrived at the Templeton house. The once proud building had already begun to fall into disrepair: the paint was peeling, and after the winter snows, the trees and shrubbery looked blasted. The yellow "For Sale" sign hung limply on a wooden stake on the front lawn, a lawn that was already showing the signs of litter, with beer cans and milkshake containers strewn about. A few windows were broken.

Beechmont thought of the Vandals of ancient times, and how they hung on the edges of civilization, waiting for it to weaken. Still, as they walked around the house in the drizzle, they too were vandals, set to break into the old house whose time had passed.

They crept around the house, testing windows and doors. Ben disappeared around a corner, then returned and said, "Psst, over here." He had found a small, broken storage-room window and had reached in and turned the lock. "I can get in here," he said, seeing himself as Secret Agent X-9 doing good by breaking in. He slid quickly through the window, slipped the catch on the door, and let in the other two.

Inside, the house was dead cold, winter still trapped within. All about them were the odors of a house where no one had lived for a time. Their voices were hushed.

"Smells musty, all right," commented Beechmont. "You got the flashlight?"

Cindy flicked the torch a couple of times.

Beechmont asked again, "Kin you remember anything else that Julia said, any repeating of a word?"

"Just those numbers," Cindy answered.

Suddenly, a tremendous "bong" rang through the house, causing the heretofore brave Burgoyne to leap for a shelf and the fearless three to jump a mile.

"The grandfather clock! My God, it's still here," hissed Beechmont. "Mebbe, just mebbe—let's have a look."

Following the waving yellow beam of the flashlight, they scurried into the gloomy front hall.

And there it stood, a magnificent reminder of a more

ordered world, still bright and proud though surrounded by the debris of a dead house. Their light glinted off its white face and intricate numbers, its arcs of sun and moon faces rolling off the chronology of life. It had, of course, stopped soon after the day of Julia Faith Templeton's death, but just now some ancient spring had suddenly uncoiled and rung out a last, resonating call—a final service from the hands of its maker.

Gingerly Beechmont knelt by the clock and tried various panels. "Lots o' these old clocks had hidey-holes for messages, particularly between lovers. Lessee—here's a little wood button." He pressed it, and with a metallic hum, a small panel opened up in the base of the clock.

Inside lay a long, white envelope. Beechmont whistled softly, "Lookee here! Let's ease her out."

Carefully he took out the envelope. Ben and Cindy leaned closer to see what the envelope contained. They were about to extract the papers contained therein when a blinding white light flooded over them.

They whirled and squinted at the glare, attempting to shield their eyes. Beechmont spoke first, his voice quavering: "You be the police?"

There was no answer, just the awful white light and the rain growling down on the roof.

"That be you, Denny Slocum? Ye always was one to come up on people." Beechmont peered at the light, hoping that behind it was Newcastle Police Chief Slocum.

Nick Tomasi held the light in one hand and a pry-bar in the other. The lawyer had said to scare them off at any cost, at any cost, he thought. Then why was his stomach in the Devil's Hell, and why was his hand shaking as he gripped the steel bar? He saw the three frightened faces, and he felt vomit coming up, when with a screaming yowl,

Old Burgoyne leapt on Nick's face, the weight of the cat bowling him over backward. The pry-bar flew uselessly in the air, and the powerful light skidded away on the floor.

As if rehearsed, Cindy grabbed the bar while Ben went after the light. She held it gingerly. Ben aimed the light at the fallen man. He lay stunned, wiping puke from his mouth, with Old Burgoyne patrolling him, growling deep in his chest. And then, unaccountably, the man half sat up and burst into tears.

The intrepid band stared increduously at the big, powerful man, his broad shoulders shaken by sobs.

Deborah Weisman was sharing a cup of tea with Michael and Helen O'Rourke in the cozy apartment over the store. She had come back for another visit for she was starved for friends, and the family seemed to like her.

Helen, who was pursing her lips, said, "Mrs. Weisman—"

"Oh please, I'm Deborah."

Helen O'Rourke thought she should smile that bright, pretty smile more often.

"Care for another cookie? You ought to—you look like you don't eat anything." Helen's motherliness was forever coming out, and she viewed this thin, bright woman like a daughter.

Deb, for her part, felt a great warmth. It had been a long time since anyone had offered her anything. She blinked and smiled.

"Miz Weisman, uh," said Mike, "we're worried about the kids. Here they are, out gallivantin' again. It's near 10:00 p.m. and rainin' like h—" (Helen silenced him with a look.) "Like heck, and they're still not home. I just don't like it."

"Hush, Mike. I'm sure Deborah is just as worried about that handsome son of hers as we are about Cindy. Aren't you, dearie?"

And Deborah, surrounded by the warmth of this family, and tea and cookies, and the obvious care of Helen, began to pour out her life—her marriage and divorce, and the move to Newcastle. She told of her job, and how recently they had tried to move her to Waterbury. But mostly she talked about Ben—her concern for him, and the difficulty they had in talking to each other. While she talked, Helen moved to the couch and put a great, comforting arm around her.

Mike, for his part, just grinned. He'd seen Helen's soothing effect all his life, ever since she had picked him out of the South Street Brawlers, dusted him off, and set him on a sturdy path.

A low hum began to insinuate itself into this family scene, growing in intensity until it reached a high, ear-boggling scream.

"Peter!" Mike O'Rourke roared.

The scream diminished to a low drone. After a pause, young Peter O'Rourke, the Electronic Marvel, sidled into the room.

"Peter," Mike bellowed, "I told you what would happen if you did that again!"

"Aw, gee whiz, I couldn't help it. The switch slipped out."

"Never mind the alibis. Go to your room. March! And I'm right behind you."

"Ah . . . oh. Hey, say dad, ya wanna know where Cindy is?" Pete asked, thinking fast and trying to avoid the spanking that was sure to come.

The adults stopped and stared at the diminutive boy.

"Well, I hear them talking all the time and I *know*

they're seeing old Beechmont and they been foolin' around old Missus Templeton's house. They can't put anything over on me!" He grinned up at his father, praying for a reprieve.

Deborah said, "Do you suppose they're up there at this time of night, in this rain?"

Helen added, "They'll catch their deaths."

"If they're not home in one half hour, I'm goin' looking for them," Mike concluded.

Pete, at this point, was sliding out of the room. Mike turned to him. "As for you, young man—"

"Yeah, Dad."

"March!"

"Aw, gee whiz!"

Earlier that day John Arnold had sat in the mayor's office, glaring at that stout worthy and thinking how he never could abide this man whose thinking was as sloppy as his whole appearance. Still, John needed him and the rest of the cheap politicians around city hall, the ones he had helped put into office. Gordy Morse, the deep-voiced mayor, could be the perfect cat's paw to settle this thing once and for all, so he had to be shown the documents.

"John, Counselor Arnold, always glad to see you," said the mayor, waddling toward him, thick hand extended. John shook it, barely touching him. "We don't see enough of you at city hall, Counselor," the mayor rumbled on.

"I try to stay away. I have as little to do with city hall as I can, Mayor."

"Siddown, siddown. Have a cigar. My doctor made me give 'em up an' he's got me on another diet." With that, Gordy swept the remains of a Snickers bar into his desk drawer. "Now, what can we do ya for?" The mayor's lips wrapped around the long, black cigar, and his tiny eyes viewed John shrewdly through the blue smoke.

"I'll get right to the point," said John. "Unless we move fast, you may find yourself the mayor of a town that doesn't exist, on land that doesn't belong to it."

The mayor smoked in silence for half a minute, then said quietly, "Ya wanna run that by me again?"

"Just this: I have proof here that Newcastle was founded on an act of violence—a murder of its rightful owner, who was in possession of a land grant of the type that is still honored in this country." And with that he banged the black metal box on the desk.

"Yer tryin' to tell me we ain't legal?" asked the mayor.

"That's right. Or the city could go broke trying to prove that we are, if the legal heir files suit against us."

"Hell, John, that's a helluva thing to say. Why, your ancestor was one of the two founders. What'd they call 'em? Proprietors. Y'mean yer great, great, great knocked off some guy and stole his land?" The mayor began chuckling at the thought of Mr. Perfection Arnold having a murderous ancestor.

John quelled an urge to reach across the desk and belt this political hack square on his bulbous nose. He said softly but with a deadly edge, "I want an emergency meeting of the city council, and I want it quickly."

"Now hold on, you ain't shown me any proof. How do I know yer playin' with a full deck?" (The mayor had missed diplomacy class in school.)

John had known he would run into this kind of attitude with Gordy Morse. In a way, he had to respect him; the fat little city executive had to have things practically shoved down his throat before he believed them. "Is your intercom turned off?" he asked.

"Yeah, an' the door's closed. Wait a minute." Gordy pressed the inter-office switch. "Miss Twitchell, no calls or anything 'til I tell you so."

John opened up the box and gingerly lifted out Gideon Templeton's sworn statement. He described the events leading up to the murder of Captain Jack Turner and concluded: "This statement appears to be in every way authentic.

"Now, let me acquaint you with a little land law," he continued. "The grant referred to is of the type that is very rare; I believe only three or four were given, but they *were* honored by the Continental Congress after the Revolutionary War. This was probably due to the fact that the Congress, recognizing that the individuals who had received these grants originally were some of the richest and most powerful men in the new nation, decreed that they would be honored in perpetuity."

"What's 'in perpetuity'?" asked the mayor.

"Forever. And it also included the heirs," John said.

"Y'mean there's someone wanderin' around that might be an heir?"

"Correct. The attendant documents attest that Captain Jack Turner had an Abenaki wife, and there was a child."

"How come no one's said anything about this before?" asked Gordy Morse. His cigar had gone out but still dangled from his mouth like a little black billy club.

"I don't know. I can only guess. The wife, who saw the murder, may not have been aware of the grant, and the child was too young to know anything," said John.

"OK, so where's this grant right now?"

For a moment, John's control left him and his hand began to tremble. He hesitated before answering, for he did not want to lose his composure in this man's presence.

"We don't have it, but I have a man searching for it. He'll find it."

"It's simple then—when you find it, just take and burn all these damn things. Anybody else know about all this?" asked the mayor.

John glanced sharply at Mayor Morse, wondering if he should tell him about the teenagers and Julia Faith Temple-ton. His dislike for the mayor clouded his perception of the man's intelligence, so he lied, "No, no one else is aware of the documents."

The mayor had relit his cigar and stared at John through clouds of acrid smoke. "It's odd that someone else don't know about all this," he said finally.

Both men stared at each other, their mistrust like a separate, silent presence in the room. Finally, John spoke: "I've checked the title deeds and record divisions of both states, Vermont and New Hampshire, and there is no record of these transactions, nor letters of transmittal. So you see, the only proof lies right before us." He did not tell the mayor of his own doubts. His own research had shown that these grants were important legal documents, so highly prized that the actual deeds were always accom-panied by letters of transmittal addressed to the governors of the territories wherein the land lay. John Arnold knew all too well that there might well be more proof, but despite his best efforts, he had so far been unable to uncover it.

"Uh, huh." The mayor, who operated on gut feelings, felt a deepening suspicion of this high and mighty lawyer. "What d'ya think we should do?"

"Summon a meeting of the executive board of the city council, the quicker the better!"

"Hold on. If we have the only proof, what's the big hurry?"

John's face reddened. "You're right, there's no hurry," he said, his voice trailing off.

Mayor Morse now knew John was lying, but he also knew there was nothing he could do about it. The mayor was just as determined as John to keep things as they were, and had no desire to change the duly constituted government of Newcastle.

Like many of the elected officials, the mayor had business dealings in the city that he did not want to see upset. Why borrow trouble? he thought.

"OK. The executive board doesn't meet until May. I'll ask for some time then. And you be there with all this stuff." Then he stood, indicating that the meeting was over. This left John in the uncomfortable position of gathering up the precious papers as the mayor gazed on impassively.

"Uh, I'll see you then," said John. But the mayor had already turned his back and was looking out the window, his round head surrounded by a cloud of acrid cigar smoke.

Nick wiped his mouth and eyes with a soiled handkerchief, looked sheepishly at the three brave adventurers, and thought: Two kids and an old wino plus a cat, geez. He hiccupped, and shivered. It was dark, cold, and damp in the mansion, and he wished he was back at Tony Pica's.

The old wino spoke (only now he didn't sound like the old wino): "I know you. You're Nick Tomasi. Kids, this guy was a right smart football player at the Catholic school."

They all fell silent, and the only sound was the wash of

rain on the roof. Then Cindy exclaimed, her voice trembling, "Y-Y-You're the one!"

Ben, his voice also quavering, added, "Right, you're the one who took the box from us. What are you doing here now?"

Burgoyne continued his silent patrol as Nick coughed and said flatly, "I was sent to find some kind of a deed."

Beechmont stepped quietly over to Cindy, took the pry-bar and held it firmly in both hands. "You'd better explain yourself, mister, right quick."

Nick looked at Beechmont in the flickering light of the flashlight. Beechmont certainly wasn't acting like a wino now. To hell with it, I'm sick of all this, he thought. He shrugged, then started to explain.

"There's a certain party in town that figures you kids know too much about certain things. This party didn't know you were in on this deal, Beechmont. Anyway, he thinks you know somethin' about this town that he don't want others to find out." Nick paused, fingering his scratched face. "I'd have included that damn cat." With this, Burgoyne paused, one paw upraised, and growled deep in his throat.

Beechmont said softly, "How come you *didn't* go for us, Nick?"

Nick blinked a couple of times, feeling moisture come to his eyes. "Ah, I couldn't. I just couldn't. I've been rotten —done some rotten things, but this . . . ah!" He sat there looking dejected.

Ben piped up, "What're we going to do now?"

Beechmont had been contemplating Nick, and finally asked him a question, one that seemed out of place considering the circumstances. "Nick, what have you been up to, I mean, since you left St. Francis?"

Something in Beechmont's tone made Nick want to talk, and talk he did. He poured out the whole story of his wandering from job to job, the loss of the airline pilot's position, the march of failure (he felt) until recently, with the jobs for "this certain party"—dirty jobs, he called them.

At the end, Ben spoke up again: "Where do we go from here?"

"Ben's right. We can't leave without resolving a few things. And I think a lot of that has to do with our friend, Nick, here," said Beechmont, looking at Nick. "As a starter, who is 'this certain party' employing you?"

"Listen, folks, I'd rather not say right now."

"OK, Nick," said Beechmont, his voice hard. "Then how do we know we can trust you?"

"That's just it. You don't know. I ain't said I'd throw in with you anyway."

"Well, will you?" Cindy inquired.

Nick glanced at the tiny girl with the big round glasses, and thought, O'Rourke, O'Rourke. My God, her father is Mike O'Rourke. We were both in the South Street Brawlers.

"Yeah, yeah, I'll help you," he said, and he felt a great weight lifted off him. It felt good, breathing.

"There's something we want to tell you," said Beechmont, and he described Ben and Cindy's suspicions about the Newcatle land grant.

During Beechmont's story, Nick's thoughts were in a turmoil. He asked himself, should he tell his new partners about John Arnold? He felt his anger turn toward the lawyer. No wonder Arnold wanted these kids out of the way. It all had to do with that box. Hell! He wished he had looked inside before delivering it. And now John Arnold thinks these kids know what's in it, Nick realized. He whistled.

"Yes, Nick?" Beechmont asked.

"No. I mean, yeah, this stuff could be dynamite. I mean, is it true?"

"Near as we can figure out it is. And you know Julia Templeton, she wasn't crazy—a little eccentric, but not crazy," said Beechmont.

"OK, listen, I'm not going to tell you who the person is that hired me—at least, not yet." He added ominously, almost under his breath, "I'll take care of that."

But Beechmont was sharp. "No rough stuff, Nick. That's out!"

"Yeah, I promise, although I can't say I'm not tempted."

During this exchange, Cindy found herself distracted by an increasing glow in the gloom. It seemed to be coming from the two narrow, etched windows by the great oak door. She rushed over and looked out. Then she dashed back to the huddled band.

"It's my father, and he's got Chief Slocum with him. Now we're in for it!" she said.

"Quick, into the secret basement room!" Ben exclaimed. "And don't forget the envelope."

Quickly they grabbed up the flashlights and made for the hidden entrance under the stairs. Ben was the last one through, and he propped the broken hallway panels over the stairwell opening as best he could before following the others down to the secret room.

As they tiptoed down the stairs, Beechmont caught sight of an old-fashioned sampler, such as children made in the olden time, on the wall of the stairwell. Good place for that old decoration to be—part of the past come back to haunt us—he thought as they huddled, barely daring to breathe, in the cold, inky blackness of the cellar room.

Meanwhile, down by Mead's Rock, Beaver Creek once again began sucking and swirling in the midst of the down-pour. It was as if all the water was being drawn toward a pool and then plunging down in a whirl, steadily wearing away the muddy banks. A train, coming up the tracks, moaning its flat, mechanical diesel horn, beamed its powerful yellow light on the base of Mead's Rock. An observer lying close to the rock would have seen some markings cut deep in the stone. But something else gleamed in the light for an instant, then disappeared as the train roared by. It was a skeletal hand, thrusting upward from the creek mud as if in supplication.

"This place smells terrible," said Chief Slocum. He flashed his powerful flashlight around the entrance hall of Julia Faith Templeton's Victorian house. "Hey, look there. I remember that old staircase from when I was a kid. We used to come here for Christmas parties. It was—"

"Listen, Denny, can we forget about the trips down memory lane. We're here to find the kids," said Mike O'Rourke. He sounded testy, but down inside he was frightened.

As they went from room to room, the flashlight beam picked up bits and pieces of a long-dead past—here an ancestral painting, somber-clothed worthies with stormy white eyes; there an exquisitely carved wainscoting: the few things left behind by the auctioneers. And everywhere was the chilly dust, puffing up in little clouds around their feet, flickering like tiny insects in the flashlight's beam. Upstairs and down, the two men poked and probed, but found not a trace of the kids.

"What about a basement? These old houses had big cellars," Mike pointed out.

"Julia had that sealed off years ago. I remember 'cause I had to direct traffic around the trucks that were hauling tons of junk out of here. Y'know, Mike, this house has been around for a long time. Why, I remember—"

"Denny, do me a favor: can the history lessons," said Mike, pausing and scratching his head. "We might as well leave. Like as not the kids will have beat us home."

"Yeah, we may as well," said Denny.

So the two old buddies shouldered out the door and into the steady rain, which was breaking up great patches of dirt-flecked snow.

Huddled in the basement, the stalwart three (plus Old Burgoyne and the tentative addition of Nick Tomasi) heard the two heavy men bumping and talking on the floor above. Most of what the searchers said was indistinguishable. Ben crept up the stairs, aided by the flashlight, and pressed his ear to the panel. When he came back down with the others he said, "They're taking off. I heard 'em say they thought we would beat them home."

"What are we going to do now?" asked Cindy.

"Wal, I think that has a good deal to do with our friend here," Beechmont said, looking at Nick.

This former football player, failed pilot, and self-confessed "dirty job" worker, ducked his head as if in shame.

There was silence in the gloom. Suddenly Cindy said,

"Look at Old Burgoyne!" The great gray cat had firmly ensconced himself next to Nick and was contentedly licking a paw.

"I guess the cat kinda gave us the answer. How about it, Nick? Is Burgoyne's judgment correct?" asked Beechmont. He was looking directly at the big man.

"Yeah, I'll do what I can," said Nick.

Beechmont asked, "What about the envelope? Did someone bring it?"

"Yeah, I got it," said Cindy.

"Let's get both lights on this," said Beechmont.

They gathered around Cindy as she opened the envelope and pulled out several sheets of paper. She spread them out, and, heads together, they read: "My name is Gideon Ivory Templeton, and having reached . . ." It was a photocopy of the entire account of the founding of Newcastle. They hurriedly read over the pages together.

Nick whistled softly. "No wonder that bas . . . the guy who sent me here wanted this stuff. It would blow the roof off this town."

Cindy said, "But look here. It says there was some kind of royal deed. The question is, where is that deed?"

"That's the $64,000 question," Beechmont said in a low voice. And that was enough to set them whispering among themselves in a quiet frenzy of conjecture.

Cindy broke in, "We better leave. I'm in Dutch already. I hate to think of what my folks are gonna do!"

Beechmont said, "OK, let's meet at my cabin one week from today. And Nick, I hope you'll be ready to tell us who the 'certain party' is."

Single file, they went up the secret stairs with Old Burgoyne climbing, then pausing, bringing up the rear.

Mike O'Rourke was in the middle of explaining the search to his wife and Deborah Weisman when all three heard the door open. It was Cindy and Ben, and who should be there to greet them, his fanny still tingling from his father's ministrations, but Peter, the Electronic Whiz Kid.

"Oooh, are you gonna get it. You won't be able to sit down for a week," he cackled gleefully.

Cindy glared. "Kid monster!"

Then they went in to face three pairs of very angry eyes.

"Young lady, just what do you think you are doing?" demanded Helen.

"Would you believe, coming home?" said Cindy, blinking owlishly behind her big round glasses.

"Young man, do you realize what time it is?" asked Deborah.

Ben looked at his mother. This was a different person —this was a mother, and boy, did she look confident.

"I . . . that is, we, ah . . . were just studying late. Ah . . . at the library." He smiled winningly, only to feel a kick on his ankle bone.

"Idiot child, the library closed five hours ago," hissed Cindy.

Deborah turned to the O'Rourkes and said, "Thanks so much for a lovely evening. Come along, young man, we have a lot to *discuss!*" Her meaning was absolutely clear, and Ben followed her out the door, mouth agape. He even forgot to throw his superiority sneer around the room.

"And now, Cynthia O'Rourke, there is one word to describe your actions for the next two weeks," her father began.

"I know—grounded!"

Later, in her room, Cindy lay on the bed staring at the ceiling. Now they'd have to postpone the meeting at Beechmont's for a week. She sighed, thinking, Where is all this going? Then she fell asleep and dreamed she was running around the library, only no one would let her in.

When Deborah and Ben got home, she put the kettle on and they sat down in the front room.

"Now, Benjamin, tell me where you've been."

Ben felt the old rage and cockiness rise. "I told you: studying. You want me to get good grades, don't you?"

"Ben, I'll ask again. Where have you been?"

He looked at this new, assured mother. The kettle whistle blew, and she rose to make herself a cup of tea. She called over her shoulder, "Would you like some cocoa?"

Now he was really confused. Here she was coming down on him, and giving him hot chocolate at the same time, he thought.

Deb returned with both cups. "Careful, it's hot." As she sipped, she looked at him expectantly.

He squirmed. Boy did he squirm. If he told her she'd blow the whistle. Breaking and entering—into the slammer for sure, for sure. He blurted, "Me and Cindy were making out."

She looked at him levelly. "That's not true. It's not even fair to your friend."

Ben's face turned crimson and he choked out, "No, I guess not!"

Deb sipped her tea, waiting.

"OK, listen, I . . we . . . we're working on . . . well, it's like a mystery. It has to do with the way this town got started. Remember that history project Cindy and I were working on?"

"Yes. I thought you had handed that in."

"We did, but there's more to it. And I can't say what it is, at least, not right now."

"All right, Ben. Now, finish your cocoa and go to bed." She paused, and almost as an afterthought said, "If I can help, just ask."

Ben lay in bed, his emotions all tangled up. He tried to untangle them with his head, but it didn't work. Funny, he used to get hot chocolate in New York. Now it's cocoa, made with milk. Vermont—cow country, he thought with wry amusement.

The next morning Nick sat in Tony Pica's nursing a beer. The first sip had tasted terrible, and he didn't know whether he could finish it. He looked around the bar at the several plywood booths with blue glass mirrors on the walls. The back of the bar itself was adorned with cardboards displaying all kinds of snacks: crackers 'n cheese, Beer Nuts, and beef jerky. The counter held jars containing pickled eggs and pigs' feet in green liquid. A dirty white can picturing a famous football player read "Give to MS." Last year's tinsel Christmas bell hung from a string over the bar. Over all was the smell of stale beer.

What a place, Nick thought. Do other people start their days in places like this? He stared at the beer and felt his stomach lurch.

Tony Pica, whose forefathers had been dispensing booze to Newcastle citizens since George Washington was a pup, shuffled amiably over and said, "Hey, Nick, what's the matter? You look like you lost it all."

"Ah, it's nothin'. Tony, how long have I been comin' in here?"

"I dunno, maybe fifteen, maybe twenty years. That's countin' before you went away," Tony said.

"Let me ask you, in all that time have I changed much?"

"Not a bit, not one bit," said Tony. He grinned broadly, thinking he had said something to cheer up his best customer.

On the contrary, this made Nick feel even worse. If only he could do one thing that would make them take notice. He thought of the kids and Beechmont; he could help them. But how? He could shoot the lawyer. What good would that do? Anyway, he'd promised Beechmont "no rough stuff."

The pay phone rang and Tony answered.

"That's for me. It's the lawyer, for sure," muttered Nick.

"Hey Nick, it's your mysterious caller."

"Nick here."

The voice on the other end was thin, dry and lifeless. It was the lawyer.

After he hung up, Nick smiled. The lawyer wanted to meet him in his office. That was a switch. Nick rubbed his unshaven face and left the bar, his unfinished beer glinting yellowishly on the counter.

A wet, smacking, early spring snowstorm had started when Nick stood in front of the yellow stone office building out of which the ancient and honorable law firm of Arnold, Leggett, Primrose, and Bourne had operated for 110 years. Nick looked up before entering, thinking that soon this group of lawyers might go right down the tubes.

He laughed without mirth. Maybe the whole damn build-ing would fall down.

When Nick entered the office, John was standing at the window. Nick addressed his back: "Yeah, lawyer, ya wanted to see me?"

There was silence in the room, broken only by the hiss of old-fashioned steam radiators. Finally, John spoke. "Nick, do you see that city down there? You and I both were born here. We grew up here."

"Yeah," said Nick. He felt like adding, So what?

"Our parents were born here, or made their way here, and prospered."

"And some lost their businesses here!" Nick said, hop-ing his sarcasm showed.

"I am well aware of how your family lost the restau-rant. I know that's the reason you dislike me. It may have been the wrong thing to do, but that's business," said John.

Was Lawyer Arnold of Newcastle's biggest law firm actually apologizing? Nick thought as he glanced at John, highly suspicious.

John turned suddenly and Nick gasped. The lawyer's face was no longer that smooth, somewhat disdainful, mask. All color had drained from it, leaving him chalk white, with dark, sunken eyes. All this contrasted weirdly with his flaming red hair.

"Jesus, you look terrible," Nick declared.

John's eyes drilled into Nick as he said, "This city is in trouble, deep trouble."

Nick sank backward into a chair, impelled by the force of the other's words.

"Here, look at these," continued John. And with that Nick found himself looking at the originals of the documents he had read the day before at Julia Faith Templeton's abandoned house. Feigning surprise, he whistled and said, "This stuff is dynamite. Does anyone else know?"

"Only Mayor Morse, and he's going to bring it up at the next meeting of the executive council," said John.

"Cripes, those windbags will have it all over town in seconds."

"I know, I know, but maybe not. They have their own interests to protect," said John.

"Listen lawyer ... uh, John, I don't understand. I mean, what can these papers actually do to the town?" asked Nick.

John's face again became terrible to behold. "It would ruin the town, the city. Think of the lawsuits, the search for heirs of this Jack Turner. What do you think the newspapers would do with it?"

Nick visualized the headlines: *CITY FOUNDED ON MURDER—Legal Heirs Sought.* Of course, families like the Arnolds, who owned large amounts of property in Newcastle, stood to lose the most if their property deeds were challenged.

"Every would-be fortune hunter and crackpot would descend on Newcastle. Ruin, I say, ruin for the town," said the lawyer. His wrath was, by now, in full focus. "I will not let it happen. By the blood of my ancestors, I won't. I will do anything, *anything,* to stop this!"

There was an awful silence in the room. Snow mixed with rain pattered against the tall windows. My God, thought Nick, I've got to stop this guy—he'd a' killed me just then if I'd been in his way.

Nick temporized, "What are you going to do?"

John calmed himself, his lawyer's logic returning.

"First of all, the executive council will have to see the documents."

"Why even show them, or why did you show the mayor? Why didn't you just burn them?" asked Nick.

"It's safer this way. By bringing in the others it will be their decision. After all, they are town government—they must make the decision. All I am is a concerned citizen who's discovered something the town council should know about. By bringing it to them, I'm just doing my duty."

Nick looked at John in open-mouthed amazement. This "concerned citizen" was going to make sure that he had the council locked into a conspiracy. He would doubtless get them to agree to destroy the papers (he probably had photostats of them already), then they'd do whatever he wanted. Unless something was done, John Arnold would be home free.

"By the way, about those kids. Is that matter taken care of?" the lawyer asked.

"Oh sure, sure. Listen, they didn't know anything. They had some kind of history paper to do, and they were poking around Miz Templeton's house illegally like I was. I don't think you'll have any trouble with them."

John stared at Nick for a long time. To Nick it seemed like hours. Finally, John spoke, "It's just as well—two dead kids might stir things up more than we need."

The last statement confirmed it for Nick. The man was a monster and he had to be stopped. And Nick, and the kids, and Beechmont, and even that crazy cat, were the ones to do it. Suddenly he felt great.

John continued, "Here is the date for the executive council meeting. I want you around. I may be needing you right after the meeting."

"OK, I'll be there."

John dismissed him by turning back to the window. Nick, on the other hand, went on his way rejoicing. He finally had a cause to fight for.

Two weeks later Deb and Ben were having dinner at home. She had taken to cooking big meals and brightening up the apartment in her new role as a confident mother. Tonight it was tuna wiggle (Deb had heard this was an old Newcastle favorite), salad, and apple crisp. Ben, for his part, groaned and tried to act disdainful as befits a sophisticated fifteen-year-old. But he gobbled up his share of food.

"Ben, I'll be going to a social workers' convention in Boston next week. I'll be gone for several days, and I've made arrangements for you to eat at the O'Rourkes. Now, I believe it will be all right for you to sleep here—after all, your books and things are here."

"Aw, Ma." The words of complaint were automatically out before he realized that this was a good deal. However, he didn't want to be too enthusiastic. "I guess that's OK. Hmm, eating at O'Rourkes, yechh!"

"My son, the martyr," teased Deb. "Oh, by the way, do you remember that old fellow, Mr. Beechmont? Why, I saw him on the street the other day and he looked just fine. All cleaned up, with the nicest little goatee. I wonder what happened?"

What happened was he got the booze out of him, Ben thought, yawning. But this got Ben to thinking about their dilemma. Here they were, sitting on dangerous information (dangerous to them), and now this Nick character was hanging around. What a bruiser he was!

Ben's mind was idling along when a fantasy of Captain Jack Turner and Rogers's Rangers began floating through his head. *He was Turner, kneeling before the king of England to receive his royal grant, then leaving England on a fast brigantine bound for America, sailing, sailing.*

Sailing! That's it! he thought. If Captain Turner had sailed back to America, there'd be records. People were always turning up records of past times. And since Boston was the port everyone sailed in and out of—

"Ma!" Ben shouted, causing Deb to spill her tea.

"Honey, I'm right here. You don't need to shout!"

"Oh, yeah. Sorry. Listen, you're going to Boston, right?"

"Yes, as I have explained."

"Well, could you go to the Hall of Shipping, or Hall of Old Records, or something, and look up some information for us . . . uh, for me?" With that Ben looked vastly mysterious.

Deborah said, "This has to do with that—business—you're engaged in?"

"Yeah," said Ben, hurrying on. "We have to find out if a Captain Jack Turner sailed on a ship called the *Lord Albermarle* around Christmas week of 1759. Also, if and when he came back, and when he arrived back in Boston, and what he had with him."

"Slow down. Write me a list, and I'll look it up." Deb had intended to go to Filene's Basement on the afternoon the conventioneers got off. Somehow, this seemed more important, though.

Mother and son resumed eating. Ben felt as brilliant as Ellery Queen, and Deborah felt like having another cup of tea—to celebrate.

Beechmont gazed around the single cozy room that made up the entirety of his dwelling, took a few puffs on his pipe, and asked, "Where's Nick?"

Cindy was wiping her glasses on the tail of her blouse. "I don't know. D'ya suppose he's told that certain party? I mean, about us?"

"Yeah," Ben chimed in. "He looked suspicious to me."

"Wal, we'll wait for a few more minutes. Now, what have we found out?" asked Ben.

Cindy began, "We know that a 'certain party' has the proof that Newcastle was stolen from Captain Jack Turner by a man named John Arnold, who killed him. We only have a copy of the testament—someone else has the original."

Ben piped up, "You remember the letters of transmittal that we read about that were always sent separately on these grants? Well, my mother is going to Boston next week, and she said she would check out shipping records and passenger lists for 1759."

Beechmont laughed, and said, "Talk about two great minds. Yesterday I wrote to the Royal Institute of Ship History in Liverpool, England. The English are great for keeping records back to the days when they painted their bodies blue and floated around in hollowed-out logs." He chuckled. "Anyway, I asked about shipping activity during the mid-eighteenth century. In other words, Ben, I'll get 'em goin', and you'll get 'em comin'."

Ben laughed. He and Beechmont had become comrades.

In the midst of all this Burgoyne had taken to prowling by the door. Suddenly his back arched and he let out a low warning growl. The intrepid band froze, and all felt the fear—a real fear that they might be in way over their heads and that they had started something they couldn't stop.

The door swung slowly open, and a huge silhouette filled the door frame. Cindy blinked rapidly behind her glasses. Ben clenched his fists to stop the trembling. Beech-mont started to get up. Burgoyne went over and began rubbing himself against the visitor's leg, and the trio relaxed.

"Sorry I'm late,' Nick said.

"Come in, come in, we ain't heating the outdoors," said Beechmont as he shepherded the younger man to a chair. "You look like you could use a drink."

"No, no, thanks. I quit that stuff a coupla days ago," said Nick, and a flash of mutual respect passed between the two men.

"OK, Nick, what have you got?" Beechmont leaned back, puffing on his pipe.

Nick sat on the edge of his chair, rubbing his hands together. Finally he blurted, "The certain party, the one who hired me, is . . . John Arnold."

The others gasped. He was talking about one of the most respected men in town. A man who gave of himself to the community. "That's the man who hired Nick to kill us?" Cindy exclaimed.

"And he has the original testament proving everything —the settling of this town, everything. I oughtta know. I stole it for him from Miz Templeton's house."

"Ole Red Arnold, wal what do ye know. But it makes sense. T'was his ancestor, John, that done the dirty deed," said Beechmont.

"What are we going to do?" asked Cindy as she looked from one face to another.

Nick said, "There's going to be a meeting of the

mayor, and John, and some other politicians. That slick lawyer has it all arranged so that the city council will make all the decisions. Let me explain ..." With that Nick outlined what had happened in John's office.

Ben said, "That'll be good. You'll be there, and you can tell us all about it."

"Not so fast, kid. I'm just an errand boy. They won't let me in on the meeting."

"But we have to know what happens in that meeting," Beechmont said.

Cindy had been sitting silently, chewing on her knuckles. Now she said, her voice barely audible, "Let's bug them."

Ben laughed. "Sounds to me like they're bugged enough!"

"I'm serious," she said. "Why can't we plant a bug, an electronic listener, in the office where they have that meeting?"

"That's a dang good idea," said Beechmont. "But just how d'ya think we can do it?"

"My brother, Pete. I hate him, but what he doesn't know about electronics is not worth knowing."

"Little genius, huh?" Beechmont paused. "You know, it sounds an awful lot like we're gettin' like them. You know, sneakin' around, plantin' bugs, schemin', and the like. I'm not so sure I like it. Then, on the other hand, I'm not so sure I *don't* like it." Having solved this moral dilemma, he stuffed his pipe full of fresh tobacco.

Ben asked, "Do you think the kid will do it—and will he keep it a secret?"

Cindy responded calmly, "If he doesn't do it, I'll kill him, and if he tells, I'll kill him again."

That seemed to satisfy everyone. Beechmont said,

"OK, let's not lose sight of each other. Ben, as soon as your mother gets back, get ahold of me, or, if my letter gets back first, I'll call you. Cindy, you handle the 'bugging.' Nick, we'll see you after the meeting. Now, let's all shake hands on it."

They all put their hands together like a basketball team, Nick's big, dark hands covering everyone's. Burgoyne strolled under this umbrella of fingers and looked up, one paw upraised.

Then the conspirators departed, leaving Beechmont puffing on his pipe.

Pete O'Rourke scooped up the last of his ice cream, setting up a tremendous rattle in the tall glass. Then he applied a straw to the last drops of sweet soda. Sucking mightily, he smacked his lips.

Cindy wrinkled her nose in disgust and said, "You sound like the ocean draining dry."

Unperturbed, Peter wiped his mouth on the back of his hand and looked at Ben and Cindy. "Now that you've bribed me, what's the job?" he inquired.

Cindy sighed. What a gross person Peter was. How could she have such a gross person as a brother?

"Listen kid, we want—" Ben began. Pete glared at Ben. "Don't call me kid just 'cause you're Cindy's boyfriend," he sneered.

"Now look, turkey—"

"Ben, please, I'll handle this," said Cindy.

She smiled sweetly at her little brother. "Peter, we both know how smart you are—I mean, all those electrical things you make."

"Yeah, stuff stupid girls don't know about." Pete was tearing a napkin into spitballs.

Quelling an urge to bash her younger brother with the napkin holder, Cindy went on. "We need your help for putting an electronic listening device in a certain place," she finished, feeling very mature.

"Ya mean a bug?" Pete exclaimed.

"Sshh, fer cripes sake," Ben hissed.

"Yes, Peter, a bug. Will you do it?" asked Cindy.

Pete look at the faces leaning toward him. Cindy added softly, "Because if you don't, I'll murder you dead."

Pete, feeling that she might very well murder him dead, readily agreed to the plot: "OK, where does it go?"

Ben said, "Never mind that. We'll show you where. And Pete—"

"Yeah?"

"If you tell anyone about this, *I'll* murder you dead."

Pete stared in wonder at the two, and began putting the spitballs neatly into an ashtray on the table.

6 THE KING'S GRANT

EARLY IN MAY, on a warm day, fog crept in and around the buildings and homes of Newcastle. As evening descended the street lights made quiet little auras above slick, black pavements. The fog curled and eddied down by Beaver Creek, touching the rising water, its quiet in contrast to the creek's springtide rush.

Beechmont had just finished reading a letter from the Royal Institute of Ships' History that verified the sailing of the *Lord Albemarle*. The passenger list included a party of American colonists and Indians led by Captain Jack Turner. Now he sat in his cabin, staring at a scrap of paper upon which was written, "Bible, the preacher, 3 and 7." He leaned back and thought of Julia Faith Templeton. The old gal is dead and she left us with a puzzle, he sighed to himself. He reached up to his crowded bookcase and brought out a worn, much-read Bible. Sitting down, he let his hand rest comfortably on it. It was like holding a dear friend. And still the dying words of Julia tumbled in his brain. He riffled the thin Bible pages. The secret was in there, but where? The book felt heavy in his hand, as heavy as the life of the world it contained.

Beechmont got up and began pacing the room. He spoke aloud, thinking that if he gave voice to his thoughts the puzzle would be solved. "Perhaps she put the deed in an old family Bible. No, it'd be too big. Maybe she hid it somewhere in the Congregational Church. That could be where the preacher comes in. Let's see, the church has three floors. Are there seven rooms on the third floor? No, it's really just one big storage room. And every church has Bibles, and there are plenty of preachers around. And all this ain't gittin' me anywhere," he finished, exasperated.

"I've got to go back up to the house, because it's still there," he exclaimed finally. As he put out his lamp and opened the cabin door, he felt a sense of strength. "Oh Julia, lead me right, old girl!"

On that very night, John Arnold had fallen asleep over a book on early Vermont land law. His sleep was shallow and fidgety. He dreamed he was running in a field, only his legs were like lead. Ahead of him loomed a huge figure, menacing, yet he still ran toward it, and it was like moving through glue. He awoke with a cry, the thick book tumbling to the floor. He was shivering uncontrollably. Someone's walking over my grave, he thought, remembering the old saying.

Getting up and going over to the sideboard, he poured himself a stiff shot of scotch, and drank, the glass rattling against his teeth. Don't worry, he told himself, nothing's going to happen—just don't worry. He peered around the room like an animal sniffing danger.

Beechmont fumbled at the broken window of the old Templeton mansion until it opened with a creak. Looking around furtively, he slowly clambered inside. He switched on his flashlight and quickly found the crossed-arrow device for the basement panel.

Gingerly he crept down the old iron stairs, his flashlight beam flicking ahead. It was darker than Billy Blue Hades, he thought. Suddenly something squirmed under his foot, causing him to come down awkwardly on the next step. It was damp and slimy, and he slipped, his whole leg plunging through the gap between two steps. The flashlight crashed to the basement floor and went out. Darkness enveloped him like a glove.

"Easy. Easy, now," he told himself as he waited for his pounding heart to quiet down. Then he tugged at his caught leg, but the space was too tight and he was trapped. Something ran over his dangling foot. "Rats. Oh, Jesus, rats, and no one knows I'm down here," he swore. Tiny, sharp teeth chattered on his boot.

"OK, old fellow, you've been in tight spots before," he muttered. Twisting his body so that he had the support of the wall, he carefully tugged and twisted until he was able, an inch at a time, to withdraw his leg. Taking no more chances on the slippery steps, he slid the rest of the way to the floor.

It was pitch black. Groping around for the flashlight, his fingers touched fur, and he heard an angry squeaking. His stomach twisted but he knew the light was his only hope.

After an eternity of feeling his way with the chittering of rats all around him, he finally touched metal. Seizing the light, he fumbled for the switch and the light went on.

Breathing a silent prayer, he flashed it all around the room until the rats, their red eyes gleaming, scurried back to their nests.

Beechmont sucked in the musty air and directed the beam to the walls. He gasped, for every bit of wall space was hung with old-fashioned samplers. There must have been over one hundred of them, in every conceivable size. Embroidered alphabets and numerals and wise sayings rested in square, oval, and rectangular frames. Several were even done in diamond shapes.

"And we didn't even notice them the last time we were here! A fine lot of detectives we are!" he whispered to himself disgustedly.

For the first time, he felt the gray clasp of discouragement. Now what am I supposed to do with all these? he asked himself. Someone must have had a lot of time on her hands, or maybe these samplers had been passed down through the generations.

He felt like he was back where he started, and all the beautiful samplers became like pieces in a jigsaw puzzle. He thought of the rats; suppose he should have a heart attack down here? He shuddered.

Beechmont swung the light around the room one more time, and was starting to leave when something caught his eye. Just to check, he turned the light back to the wall of samplers. It picked out a large, square one with much needlework. But the word that leapt out at him, held steady in the flashlight beam, was, *Ecclesiastes*.

At that moment he knew he had found what he was looking for. "Oh Julia, you were clever, savin' this thing until the right moment, hidin' it so only some God-fearin', Bible-readin' old soak could find it. And who's the old preacher in the Bible?" he exclaimed aloud. His light fell square on the sampler, on the delicate needlepoint that spelled out, "Ecclesiastes—the Preacher of the Bible." The bright yellow glow illuminated the wrought needlework:

> *To Every Thing*
> *There Is a Season,*
> *And a time to Every*
> *Purpose Under Heaven*
> *Ecclesiastes 3:7*

"The numbers were the clue, eh Julia," murmured Beechmont. "'A Time to Rend, a Time to Sew.' Must have taken you a right long time to sew this up. 'A Time to Keep Silent.' Hard on you, eh Julia? Always knew you as a talker. 'And a Time to Speak Out.' And now's the time. Good goin', Julia!"

Taking the sampler from the wall, he climbed carefully up the basement stairs, taking care to stick close to the passage wall. Reaching the hall, he turned the sampler over and carefully began to take off the stained cardboard backing.

Soon the back was off, and under it was a large piece of very fine linen. Beechmont turned this back like a coverlet on a bed, then let the powerful beam from his flashlight play over his discovery. Tiny sparks of light danced back to him from gold leaf laid on this parchment over two hundred years ago. The calligraphy was bold and fancy, and waxen seals gleamed dully in the gloom.

It was a blaze from the past, the script so elegant, graceful, and complicated as to make it nearly unreadable. There was the kingly seal in purple wax, royal ribbons framing the foaming calligraphy, and on top, the great emblem of England—the lion and unicorn fiercely guarding heraldic glory. Beechmont could envision the wigged and perfumed court, the bedchamber intrigues, the armies of the empire marching and fighting through an alien wilderness—all of this encompassed in the magnificent parchment.

And smack in the middle was Captain Jack Turner's name. It was the royal land grant, and it proved the Gideon Templeton account beyond the shadow of a doubt.

Beechmont shook himself from his reverie. It was time to get out. He put the cover and cardboard backing on the sampler frame, made sure the basement panel was shut, and left the house. A short time later, he was walking down Spruce Street when Police Chief Dennis Slocum spotted him and pulled over in the cruiser.

"Hey, Beechmont, whatcha doin'?"

"Well, Denny, how be ye? I'm jest taking a little stroll."

"I'm glad I ran into you," said the chief. "I've been meaning to tell you how good you're lookin' these days. Why, I haven't had to run you in since last fall."

"Stopped drinkin', I did. Do ye miss me?" Beechmont's eyes twinkled.

Chief Slocum tried to look solemn, but secretly he was pleased at his old friend's appearance. "What you got there?" he asked.

"Oh this—ain't it a beauty? Old lady Walbridge was cleanin' out her attic and give it to me. It's an old-fashioned sampler," he said, holding it up under the street light so Chief Slocum could see.

"Pretty nice, pretty nice. Well, I got to get goin'. I'll see you around," he said. And with that he jumped into the cruiser and squealed off down the street.

Beechmont continued on his journey, one hand clutching the sampler, the other jammed deep in his pocket to hide the trembling.

Later Beechmont sat dozing in his cabin when he awoke to a call, or at least he thought he heard his name being called. It echoed in his mind, like someone way outside the cabin had been summoning him. He sat up in the rocker, his heart pounding. The lamp had gone out, and an eerie glow flooded through the window.

Shrugging on his rain jacket and pocketing a small flashlight, he went out. All around him the fog glowed, a greenish-gray nimbus. He walked toward Beaver Creek, toward Mead's Rock. Strangely, he felt no fear as he drew near the big granite outcropping. He knew this ground well, but still it was a dangerous time to be climbing over the slippery rock near the creek: melting snow and ice from the mountains made the creek a treacherous beast, ready to snatch the unwary for drowning. Beechmont continued his trek through the glowing fog. Kneeling by the rock, which loomed hugely above him, he flashed his light at its base.

The creek bank had worn away, revealing "new rock," brighter than the weathered portions above it. The light flickered, and it was then that Beechmont saw a gleam of white. Bending closer, as a particularly strong rush of water swept at the white thing, he saw it was a skeletal hand, intact—real and yet unreal.

Beechmont felt a great surge of emotion in his breast as he took the ghostly white hand in his. He wept with an age-old grief.

The flashlight had fallen on the muddy bank, and its beam was fixed on the great rock. Circled by the yellow-white light were markings, clear and gleaming, scratched into the base of the ledge. Beechmont reached to pick up the flashlight. Instead, he found himself staring directly at the rock markings. He leaned closer, as if to burn the carvings into his mind, then abruptly picked up his torch and went home.

Back in the cabin, shaking the damp from his clothes, Beechmont reached high on his bookshelves and plucked a slim, tattered volume from the stacks. It was titled *Indian Pictograms of New England.* Swiftly he committed the carvings (so fresh in his mind) to paper, and began the laborious job of translating them.

By morning the fog and rain had cleared, and a dawn of surpassing beauty tinged the skies. Beechmont stood in the doorway of his cabin, breathing the fresh morning air. His smile was sad and yet relieved. He said softly, to no one, "We have the proof we need." Gazing at the distant Beaver Creek, he mused, "But what happened to the boy?"

Two nights later three shadowy figures crept up to city hall. Reaching the back door, they paused. In fact, Ben, who was in the lead, stopped so suddenly the others piled up on him.

"Look out, dummy!"

"Quiet—sshh!"

"How'd I get mixed up with these two stumblebums?" This last came from Peter O'Rourke, the Electronic Whiz Kid, looking heavenward appealingly. He was loaded down with electronic paraphernalia.

"Ya got the stuff?" asked Ben.

"Naw, this is black spaghetti and these little round things are black meatballs!" Again Pete rolled his eyes toward heaven.

"You sure the back door is open?" Cindy hissed.

"Sure I'm sure," said Ben. "The janitor leaves it open so he can sneak out for a quick beer."

The three entered the back door and found themselves in a high-ceilinged hall with offices opening on each
side. The hall itself ran clear through to the main entrance
on Lincoln Street. Most of the downstairs offices belonged
to the police and motor vehicle departments. It was the
upstairs they were interested in, particularly the mayor's
office.

This office was reached by a broad stairway curving up
off the main hall. They began the ascent, pausing occasionally to listen for Herby, the janitor. Gaining the upper
floor, they slunk by the glass-enclosed city council
chambers and down to the mayor's office. It was a corner
office (as befitted his station), and the door was half open.

"Hist, Cindy! Nick said the meeting was going to be in
here?" asked Ben.

"Yeah, they want it private. Peter, where are you going
to put the, uh ... thing?" she asked.

"I dunno yet."

They looked around the gloomy office. It was filled
with the trappings of political life: pictures of smiling
politicians, awards, and cartoons. A green marble desk sign
proclaimed "Mayor Gordon Morse," and the room reeked
of stale tobacco. Incongruously, the office was filled with
hanging plants. This was the influence of Mayor Morse's
diminutive wife, Biscuit, who had spent a lifetime offering
her pudgy solon the finer points of civilized living. The
office plants represented one of her few successes.

"I got it!" Pete whispered.

"Got what?" the others whispered back.

"Where to put the bug." Taking a tiny piece of wire,
Pete deftly looped it around the green leaf of one of the
hanging plants. On this he affixed a microphone no bigger
than a button.

"Now listen, you two," he said, savoring his moment of command. "That bug is also a transmitter." Figuring he was dealing with total ignorance, he went on methodically, "That means that it'll not only pick up the voices, it'll send them out. You understand?"

The others nodded—dumbly, Pete thought.

"When's the big meeting?" he asked.

"Nick said next week," Cindy answered.

"It better be, 'cause the battery in this thing is only good for eight days. And you better have the tape recorder close to the building—it doesn't transmit very far."

The others nodded. Then Cindy reached into her jacket pocket and pulled out something, half hiding it behind her.

Ben said, "What's that?"

"It's a sign," Cindy said, sounding defensive.

"Huh?"

"Well, I got to thinking that everyone's sneaking around and doing dishonest things. I mean, look at us," she said.

"Yeah, but we're the good guys," Ben said.

"Anyway, I made this sign, and I'm going to put it in the plant." With that she pulled out a small cardboard cut-out of a beetle that had lettered on its carapace, "This Is A Bug."

"Whaaat?" Ben and Pete nearly screeched. *Whaaat* was all they could say seconds later when, mewing prettily and tripping delicately, Herby's city-hall cat, Algernon, headed directly into the mayor's office.

"Aarrgh," grunted Ben.

But they froze again, for this pampered pet was followed by the voice of Herby, long-time city hall janitor.

"Algie, sweetie puss, where are you? Daddy's got din-din. Come on, sweetie." With that he set up a falsetto, "Kitty, kitty, kitty, kitty."

All three groaned. Obviously Herby had been visiting Tony Pica's, for they could hear him stumbling around. But their hearts were in their throats, for the stumbling was coming toward them.

"Kitty, kitty, kitty. Where are you, you damn cat?"

By this time Algernon, all sugar and twinkling whiskers, was circling the conspirators, mewing and blinking his pink-rimmed eyes.

Cindy sang softly, "We're gonna get caught, just you wait and see!"

Ben finished the song, "How come everybody's pickin' on me?"

Pete edged away from them, having acquired a deep belief that he was dealing with two loonies.

Herby lurched closer. "Did snookums go into the mayor's office? Mean ol' Gordy Morse. Won't give ol' Herby a raise." And the janitor made a noisy, wet raspberry in the general direction of the mayor's office.

By now Herby had reached the door, and the kids were huddled behind the big desk.

There was a low growl behind them, followed by a screaming yowl, and the gray shape of a large, muscular cat flung itself out of the shadows and pounced upon the delicate Algernon. This sissy cat shrieked and jumped a foot in the air, all paws and white fur extended.

But there was no escape. The gray seized the white by the scruff and walked him out the door, depositing him at Herby's feet. Then, with a flourish of tail, he darted up the hall and disappeared down the stairwell.

"Poor baby. Awwwww, mean ol' cat hurt 'um? We'll go get some din-din." And Herby shuffled down the stairs, still murmuring, with Algernon in his arms, still mewing.

The conspirators stood up.

"Whew, saved! Where'd that cat come from?" asked Pete.

For once his older companions could act superior. "That was Old Burgoyne. That cat is weird," said Ben.

"Well, I'm glad he's weird. He sure knows when to arrive on time," Pete said.

They padded softly out of city hall and out into a new spring night. Back in the mayor's office the big hanging plant swung slightly, a little sign planted among the stalks, a little sign shaped like a beetle.

John Arnold had not been idle. His thoughts had been of Captain Jack Turner's child. Templeton's account had recorded the fact of a wife and an infant. Old John hadn't been able to slaughter them. The lawyer smiled, grimly. He felt like a man caught in a tide—there was no turning around or swimming against it. He had to see it to the end.

Shaking off his reverie, he contemplated the unopened letter in front of him. It was a neat, green envelope with a return address printed in colonial-style type, spelling out "New England Society for the Descendants of Rogers's Rangers." Opening the letter, he read:

Dear Mr. Arnold,

In response to your letter of April 17, we hope the following information will be helpful to you.

The movements of Captain Jack Turner (known on the New England frontier of mid-eighteenth century as "Scouter") were fairly well recorded during the height of the Rangers' skirmishes in the Grants and elsewhere. (I have enclosed a record of the movement of Rogers's Rangers between 1750 and 1760.) In late 1759, it appears that Jack Turner was sent as an emissary of General Jeffrey Amherst to the court of George III. He was also placed in charge of a large group of individuals and products indigenous to the New England of mid-eighteenth century. The reasons for this expedition have remained obscure; however, some historians suspect that this was an eighteenth-century method of reporting to the boss!

In any case, Captain Turner returned, having married one of the Abenaki women in the entourage, and, according to suppliers and tavern records of the day, headed toward the western section of the New Hampshire Grants. In fact, Mr. Arnold, his destination appeared to be lands that constitute your community—present-day Newcastle!

At this point, we were unable to locate any further trace of this redoubtable frontiersman. This is not surprising, for the Rangers were afflicted with an itch to explore, and many rejoined Major Robert Rogers as he continued his search for the Northwest Passage to the Orient.

Your generous check has made it possible to continue the investigation surrounding the peregrinations of Captain Turner's wife.

Her name is recorded as Kohega, and she was the daughter of an Abenaki chief who was known as a statesman among the New England and New York Algonquins, and who served as a mediator between warring factions of both his own and other Indian nations. In any case, he disowned his daughter for her marriage to a white man, a Ranger. (You will remember that the Ranger massacre at Saint Francis—Lake Memphremagog—had infuriated the Indian tribes as no other English depredation had. The Rangers in particular were hated for this deed.) Therefore, if and when Captain Turner left her and their infant, she could not have returned to her people.

According to our resource in your area, a young Abenaki woman and infant boy appeared on a spring day in 1764 at the home of the Reverend Dean Irving Walker, Pastor of the Sanctity Congregational Church. This worthy took in the obviously distraught mother and sheltered her and her child.

This information, by the way, is available in the Pittsford (Vermont) Historical Society Museum. This little community is only six miles away from Newcastle. I am sure, for obviously you have a great interest in matters historical, that you will be delighted to pore over the writings of the prolific Reverend Walker.

You'll forgive my enthusiasm, but we do not often find our historical detective work rewarded so handsomely.

Briefly, the Reverend Walker raised the child (Jeffrey), and taught the mother the goodly duties of an obedient eighteenth-century woman (somewhat different from our day and age, eh, Mr. Arnold?). For reasons unexplained, Kohega (the Abenaki mother) insisted that her son take the name of the Reverend Walker and so become Jeffrey Walker.

He appears to have grown to manhood, married, and stayed in your area. In fact, the old church records show no major movement of the Walkers from that community.

Who knows, there are probably direct descendants of Jeff Walker living right in Pittsford, or perhaps right in your own town.

I have not sent you complete details as I know you will want to examine the old records for yourself.

If I can be of further help, please let me know. Good hunting (historical, I mean).

Yours sincerely,

Zachariah Abernathy
Secretary

John regarded the letter with distaste. Good hunting, indeed, he thought, and felt the bile rising in his belly. He didn't need to travel to Pittsford to get the picture. Any direct descendants of Captain Jack Turner probably still lived here.

Picking up the county telephone directory, he counted quickly. There were fifty-one Walkers living in Newcastle County. "Which one, or which ones?" he asked himself, stabbing his letter opener harder and harder against the desk.

Beechmont was again sitting at his table, reading the translation of the Mead Rock carvings. It was beautifully and brutally simple, like life on the frontier.

CAME IN
RAIN

TO OUR HOUSE

STAYED ONE
NIGHT

A MAN

WENT BACK
IN FOREST

CAME BACK
IN NIGHT

KILLED

MY HUSBAND

I RAN

STAYED IN FOREST
FOUR NIGHTS

CAME BACK

X X X X
X X X X
HOUSE GONE

BURIED MY HUSBAND

HUSBAND
IS

JACK

I LEAVE WITH SON

NEVER SEE PLACE
AGAIN

Beechmont pondered this tragic little tale. Where did they go? Did they perish in the forest? Did the boy grow up to marry? Have kids? Did some of the heirs live around here?

He sighed. Having unlocked one door, they now were faced with another mystery. He supposed he could do research at the library, or go to Montpelier, or write a thousand letters to Boston or Washington, or ... Suddenly Beechmont was tired. He lay down and fell asleep instantly —and dreamed he was walking out of a deep green forest into a white, all-enveloping mist. It was not an unpleasant dream, and he slumbered on.

On that very day, Ben Weisman came home from school and found his mother unpacking. She was back from her conference in Boston.

"Hi, Ma!"

She whirled, and for a moment Ben was amazed. His mother looked absolutely beautiful. She glowed. Ben was silent, but she rushed to him and kissed him gaily.

"Ben, I missed you, but I had fun!" she said.

This announcement put Ben's nose out of joint. He hadn't been having any "fun," he thought.

"Great," he said sourly.

But Deborah ignored him as she rattled on about her trip. They went to two plays and a nightclub, and she saw old friends (Ben sullenly noticed that his mother's cheeks were pink when she mentioned this circumstance), and they went to the aquarium. (Ben wondered if they got any work done.) "And, by the way, my friend and I—he helped —went to the Boston Museum's Maritime Hall. We looked up your question. Now let me see, I wrote it down here somewhere."

Cripes, what's happened to my organized mother? Ben thought.

"Oh, here 'tis! OK, a ship o' the line, I guess that means a warship, named *Lord Albemarle* left Boston Harbor on New Year's Eve, 1759, and set sail for Portsmouth, England, carrying a large contingent of passengers plus all manner of goods: woven cloth, arrowheads, native pottery, all kinds of corn and wheat flour, and vegetables.

"And there were a lot of Indians along, soldiers, Rangers—a real mixed bag. The passenger list was lengthy. I listed them down; Roger helped. There were (besides the captain and the crew), a Captain Jack Turner (he was the leader, I guess), Lieutenant William Phipps, Rangers Whitney, Shortsleeves, Betit, Cooper. Here's an interesting name, an Abenaki—is that the way you pronounce it?— a woman called Kohega. Here's an Indian chief. These women may have been chaperones: goodwives Cholomedly, Pettibone, Smith, and North."

She's having a ball, and I feel like I need a Tums, ruminated Ben.

"Now, this same warship returned to Boston about two years later with pretty much the same load of people. There were a few names missing, probably died over there or en route. Roger and I spent the whole afternoon in the Maritime Hall," she said brightly.

I'll bet, thought Ben gloomily.

"Anyway, this Captain Turner was part of the ship's company, and he must have married that Indian lady, because she's listed on the return voyage as Kohega Turner, and she's also listed as "greate with childe." You know how they spelled in those days, with an *e* at the end like, *greatee with childee.*"

Ben groaned like a martyr.

"The *Lord Albemarle* sailed from Portsmouth in a large convoy, but a terrific mid-Atlantic storm sank all but the *Lord Albemarle*. It was the only one to arrive safely in Boston."

Now Ben had his answer. That was why no records of the grant had come to light before: the letters of transmittal had gone down with another ship. Suddenly Ben brightened. He even felt a little pleased that his mother was happy. He stared at her like a beagle and mumbled a thank you.

John Arnold drove the few miles north to Pittsford, unaware of the delicate beauty the northern spring was bringing to the land. He sped by wild buckwheat and bleeding heart, and the birds promising a softer climate in days to come. Instead, turned inward, he chewed over the circumstances that had brought him to this point. He had a growing feeling that an heir to Jack Turner did still live hereabout. His thoughts jumped to Nick—he was suspi-

cious of Nick. Over the years their relationship had involved deeds that would not stand up under the impartial
(and glaring) light of the law. He didn't know whom he
hated more, himself or Nick. They both knew too much.
He drove on, feeling bitter and sour.

Perched lightly on her tall stool with the low bucket-
swivel seat, Dorothy Golightly surveyed the general room
of the Pittsford Museum through pince-nez bifocals bal-
anced precariously on the end of her nose. How she loved
it here. Each painting, each piece of furniture and old
book, was like a dear old friend to her.

Dorothy, who was seventy-six years old, had been taking care of the museum for fifty years. She was so thin that
a person could almost see through her, but when it came to
matters of Pittsford history her energy was boundless and
her knowledge encyclopedic.

She heard a car pull up in front. That would be the
lawyer fellow, she thought. She had remembered him when
he called, for he was the same one Mr. Abernathy of the
New England Society of Descendants of Rogers's Rangers
had written her about. This should be interesting.

The door opened with a tinkle of its little bell, and
Dorothy Golightly saw a medium-built young man with
bright red hair and an angry set to his eyes.

"Mr. Arnold, I presume."

"Yes, Mrs. Golightly, I spoke to you on the phone."

"Yes, yes indeedy, and welcome to our museum." She
smiled benignly.

"Uh, yes, of course. Now, can we get on with it?"

Dorothy was startled at first by his abrupt manner, but
with the wisdom of age, forgave him. He was probably a
busy young lawyer.

"Why yes. I hope I have not been presumptuous, but I

have brought out the old Walker Bible and attendant diaries and records. They are in the Walker Room. Here, I'll show you. Praise be to God, Pittsford had a minister like the Reverend Dean Irving Walker as one of its founders. How that man loved to record things!" she continued. "Anyway, here we are, and I'll just leave you alone to your research. Oh, would you like a cup of tea? I was just making some."

"Well," John's demeanor was softening. "Sure, that'd be fine." And with that Dorothy closed the door softly.

Turning to the books, John was at first impressed by the weight and design of the old Bible: the faded gilt devices and furbelows, the delicate pages edged in brown, and a cover soft as dust.

And what he was looking for was noted in the book—a clear family history brought up to about 1927. Noted in small, neat numbers were references to a diary or journal. John gingerly opened this small, worn black diary, crumbling with age. He read:

April 15, 1764: There came to the parsonage this evening an Indian woman with an infant. She was distraught and full of ill humors. The child appeared robust, albeit squalling in the manner of infants. We took her in, with my good wife Martha ministering to mother and child.

(Later.) A remarkable circumstance: The Indian woman is quite versed in English. She told us a tale of true horror, of her husband being murdered and the fact of her flight. We shall certainly look into this matter in the morning.

We finish this entry under the blessing of God and ask that the Supreme Being grant us wisdom and guidance in the events now set before us.

Weather: Winds from the northwest. Temp. 45°. Gen'l conditions: blustery and clear.

April 27, 1764: Having departed the parsonage early this morning, and accompanied by the Abenaki Indian woman, Kohega, we arrived at the place where her husband had met his horrible death. Amazing! There was no trace of murder, or, indeed, of the small farm and buildings that had been their home. However, so accurately did she describe the foul deed, and show me exactly where the cabin was, and where sat the goat pen, that I have no choice but to believe her.

Further down the creek we saw a new farm with buildings under various stages of construction. Cautioning the young woman to remain, I went to this farm but no one was about. After much halloo-ing, I returned to my charge. And seeing her again after just a short time apart I was struck by her innocence and brightness. Her guilelessness and honesty shone forth in the forest clearing, quite unlike some parishioners of my church, who profess Christian faith and love but sharp their neighbors, calling it sound business practice! How close to God I felt as this wonderful child told me of her life in the forest glade. You may be sure the Walkers will do right by this young woman and her child.

Weather: Calm with light breezes. Temp. 60°. Gen'l conditions: Bright and warm.

John read on, fascinated by the pastor's thoroughness. Recorded in the diary was the integration of Kohega into the Walker household, the giving of Walker's name to the child (who became Jeffrey Walker), and so on and so forth. The diary's last entry was in 1770, in December.

... and so my chest feels tight and croupy. My limbs are without strength, and I may be in the condition of meeting my Maker. Good wife Martha frets about me. She has been a joy and a blessing to me all these years. Soon it will be Christmas, the Advent of our blessed Lord upon this sorrowing orb. I ask His blessing on this household and to our wards, the Indian woman Kohega and her little son, Jeffrey, who has taken my name. God bless all in our congregation as I prepare to take leave of it. I commend my soul to the Everlasting.

Weather: Winds from the west. Temp. 31°. Gen'l conditions: snow.

A valuable book, he thought—the family tree goes back to the 1600s. Tracing carefully along the faded brown ink, he discovered that young Jeffrey married a Rachel Williams and had two children. The daughter died at age five, and the son Robert married Abigail Fox. They had one child, Bruce, and so on down the family tree.

John's interest quickened as he read. They were great ones for having one- or two-children families, and most of them died out. However, it looked as if the bloodline extended right down to ... "Irving Walker married D'Arcy Pomainville, and their issue was one child, a boy born in 1925," he read. Both parents were listed as having died in 1927. Here the genealogy ended, except for the name of Irving and D'Arcy's child.

The name was Beechmont.

John looked up, murmuring to himself, "Beechmont. Unusual. Where have I heard that name before?"

The door opened softly behind him.

"Mr. Arnold, would you like more tea?"

"Oh, thanks. I'm just about done here."

They settled around a Spode tea service, and Dorothy poured the straw-colored tea into cups. "Lorna Doone?" she asked, offering the cookies.

"Mrs. Golightly, how much do you know about the Walker family?"

"Oh, it's an old Pittsford family, but let me tell you, it's about died out."

"Are there any heirs, ah, that is, any Walkers still living around here?"

"No real Walkers, that is descendants of the saintly Reverend Walker," she said. She sighed and took a sip of tea. "You see, he, God bless him, never had natural children. That was why he gave his name to the little Indian boy. *His* descendants became the Walkers of Pittsford. It's all in the Bible, recorded by all the preachers that came after Reverend Walker. Another cookie?"

"So the line has pretty well died out, eh?"

"We don't know for sure. There was a boy born to Irving and D'Arcy, poor dears, they were both drowned in the flood of twenty-seven and the boy disappeared. I think he was drowned, too. Name of Beechtree, or Beechcliff, or something like that."

"Beechmont."

"Yes, d'ye know of him?"

"No, not really. His name was in the Bible."

"Oh, of course, how forgetful of me."

As John drove south, the name kept ringing in his head. Beechmont, Beechmont—where had he heard it? Then it came to him so suddenly he had to veer to avoid oncoming traffic: the old wino. That character that panhandled all over town—was it him? How could it be that old drunk? Still, no one knew where he came from.

His jaw set grimly, John drove on, spring-green bushes stirring in his automobile's wake.

Like a scorpion, winter in Vermont never leaves without flicking the landscape one more time with its icy sting. Today, as the intrepid detectives met in Beechmont's cozy cabin, every building and tree dripped with heavy, wet snow, looking incongruous against the lovely green leaves.

And so they gathered: Beechmont puffing on his pipe and tending a big pot of tea, Cindy and Ben poring over the royal grant, Nick nervously leaning against the door frame, and Old Burgoyne dozing by the railroad stove, opening a judicious eye from time to time.

"This gives us all the proof we need, doesn't it, Beechmont?" Ben said, shifting the great deed on the cabin table.

Cindy interrupted, "Not so. It looks like an authentic grant all right, but there is nothing that ties it to Newcastle 'cept the part in those papers that talks about the surveyor's map. And we don't have that."

"Smart girl," said Beechmont. "All we have is copies of the old Templeton report."

"So the lawyer has the rest of the proof," finished Ben.

Cindy said, "It's like having one half of a secret message—it's no good until you have the other half."

As the brave band contemplated the dilemma, the silence was like something you could touch.

After a few minutes Beechmont spoke: "Now we know John Arnold is plotting to remove any evidence that this here royal grant exists."

Cindy said, "I don't care if he is the best-known lawyer in town, he's not going to scare us." Her lip trembled a little bit, though.

Ben chimed in, "He can't scare us. All lawyers are a bunch of crooks anyway!"

"What about it, Nick?" Beechmont asked, turning to him. "You've been around him quite a bit. What do you reckon he'll do?"

Nick came out of his fitful reverie. He spoke slowly, his voice a record of warning. "That guy is pure danger. I don't trust him. I think he's gone around the bend."

"What do you mean?"

"I dunno—I just dunno," was all Nick could say.

Beechmont slowly put down his pipe and turned to the teapot. "Tea's about steeped. Who wants some?

Nick started forward impatiently, so suddenly that the kids gasped and Burgoyne was on his feet, growling.

"Didn't you hear me, old man? He's liable to do *anything!*" Nick's voice was harsh and cracked.

"What are *you* going to do, Nick?" Beechmont's voice was low and soft.

"I . . . I don't know." Nick looked down at his great hands. "You don't understand. He could help me get back on the airlines—to being a command pilot. And the breaks —they said I had a heart murmur. They grounded me, and I ain't been the same since." He stopped, sighing, and realized the tears were rolling down his cheeks—just like a stupid, stupid, stupid baby, he thought. He plunged on: "I done rotten things for that lawyer, but I can't blame him —I done them. And now, here's a chance, a chance to be a man again, and . . ." Nick stopped talking. He was breathing heavily and his face was flushed.

Beechmont met his gaze levelly and again asked, "What are you going to do?"

Nick just stared dumbly.

Beechmont gauged the younger man for a moment, then said, "Nick, supposin' this lawyer thinks I'm involved; then he'd order you to kill me, right?" Beechmont went on without waiting for a reply. "If you did that, you'd have to kill the kids, and then you'd have to kill Burgoyne, there. From what I know of that old cat, I don't think he'll put up with it."

The scene was frozen for an instant. Then Cindy, reaching for Burgoyne, began to laugh. Ben started grinning, Beechmont began chuckling, and finally Nick joined in. They laughed uproariously at the thought of the big man and the golden-eyed cat in a battle royal. The tension broken, Burgoyne retreated to a corner, glaring balefully at these crazy humans.

As the laughter quieted, Nick wiped his eyes and said, "Goddam, old man, you're too smart for me."

"Wal, maybe I knew ninety percent of it—it's that ten percent that'll kill ya." And they all fell to laughing again.

Later, as they sipped tea, they shared the information gathered so far. Ben told of his mother's trip to Boston, how she had found out that the ship carrying the letters of transmittal for Jack Turner's royal grant must have been lost at sea.

Then Ben and Cindy looked at each other, hesitated, and said almost in unison, "We've got something else to tell, too."

"Don't tell me Julia Templeton's ghost has come back!" Beechmont chuckled.

Cindy stuck to business. "Nick, is that meeting of the town's high muckety-mucks going to be soon?"

"In a couple of days."

"Good, 'cause the bug is now planted in the mayor's office," said Ben.

"An electronic listening device," added Cindy, quoting Pete. "I hope the meeting *will* be in that office after all."

Nick assured the crew that it would be.

Beechmont said, "It looks like we're all set, then. But the question is, all set for what?"

Cindy bubbled, "To tell the truth! I mean, about the town and who it really belongs to after all. Captain Turner had a son, so maybe—" she stopped and stared at Beechmont.

"You thinkin' what I'm thinkin'?" asked Beechmont, putting down his pipe.

"You mean, that the lawyer thinks there's an heir still around—someone who actually owns Newcastle but doesn't know it?"

"Right."

Ben laughed. "That means anyone around here or anyplace in the world could be the rightful heir. Even you, Beechmont. Heck, you've been around here long enough."

But Cindy picked up on this and said, "Just suppose, for example, Beechmont *was* the heir. We'd have to get proof.

"Beechmont—everyone calls you that, but don't you have a last name?"

"Yes, it's Walker. I was raised at the old Pettibone Orphanage, and they all called me Beechmont there. I joined the Navy right out of high school, and when I was discharged I came right back here. Didn't know no other place to go. And I just stopped using my last name."

Beechmont paused and cleared his throat before continuing. "And that ain't all . . ." He stopped, bowed his head, then looked up. Tears glistened in his eyes as he resumed, "Lately, I've been havin' dreams—dreams about bein' in the woods and bein' attacked. And I've had some queer feelin' that old Jack Turner is—well, part of me."

Cindy suddenly felt a desire to rush over and put her arms around her old friend, but instead she just asked gently, "Weren't you ever curious about your ancestors?"

"Wal, no. Ain't that funny? I got more lore about Newcastle and the great state of Vermont around here," he said, waving toward his floor-to-ceiling bookshelves, "and I don't have anything about myself!"

"Do you think there are records somewhere—at the orphanage?" asked Ben.

"The Pettibone Orphanage burned down in 1952, and all the records with it. Some say it was mysterious circumstances. I dunno."

"Is there anyplace else?" wondered Ben.

Beechmont started thumbing through the copied documents from Julia Faith Templeton, and paused at the section where Gideon Templeton described the existence of a wife and child. Where could they have gone, assuming they hadn't been killed? Gideon Templeton had mentioned reports of an Indian woman and child living north of the settlement.

Stepping to his bookshelves Beechmont pulled down a dog-eared tome entitled *Maps and Dates: Vermont Before It Was Vermont.* Opening to the map depicting the Newcastle area in 1764, he noticed the tracery of a trail leading to a small settlement called Pittsford about eight miles north of Newcastle. He then turned to an index of early settlers and looked under Pittsford. The names read: Andrew Pitt (believed to be the first settler); Aaron Samuelson; Charles Shaker; Joseph Pecor; D.I. Walker, a minister; Jedediah Wilson. A preacher. Maybe that was it, Beechmont thought. After all, the testament said Captain Turner's Indian wife had converted to Christianity. Perhaps she'd have gone to a minister when she was homeless.

Ben said, "Hey, Beechmont, remember us?"

"Huh? Listen, I have a hunch about this. If Turner's wife, Kohega, traveled north, she might have reached a little settlement called Pittsford. (It's still there, of course.) If she got there with her little baby, perhaps someone took her in. Now, they've got a museum up there. There's a lady at the museum. What's her name—been there forever—

funny name. Oh yes, Dorothy Golightly. It might be worth a trip to see what she knows."

Ben asked, "How're we going to get there?"

"Since I'm the only one with a car, I guess I'm elected," Nick answered.

"Great!" Cindy said, excited at the prospect of more detective work.

"Hold on," Beechmont said, tapping out his pipe. "No need for all of us to go pilin' up there. Probably scare the poor old dear out of her wits. Jest a couple of us. Cindy, you and me'll go on up tomorrow. We'll look for old church Bibles; they're good for birth, death, and marriage records. Also old town records," he said, rubbing the pipe bowl on the side of his nose. "Y'know somethin', we're all gettin' pretty good at this.

"Nick, will you give us a ride there and drop us off?" He paused, looking at Nick. "Somehow I don't think it'd be a good idea for you to be near the museum."

Burgoyne, feeling the call of nature, scratched at the door until he was let out. Evening was coming on the town, and everywhere it dripped winter's last snowstorm.

Beechmont watched the last of them struggle up the riverbank, away from his cabin. He fancied that the big gray cat had deliberately glanced back at him, golden eyes sparkling.

Calmly he went into the cabin and found a shovel. Following the trail, he headed to Mead's Rock, where he had left the remains of his ancestor after seeing the carvings on the rock. Digging carefully, he slowly began to uncover the ancient bones. He worked through the night, handling the remains as if they were the most precious ivory, wrapping each bone in fresh cloth. When he was finished, he carried the relics to his cabin. A misty spring dawn rewarded his labors, and he slept deeply with a silent sweetness that matched the morning.

A few days later, Dorothy Golightly sat contemplating the pale blossoms on a bush that grew just outside a side window of the Pittsford Historical Society Museum. Adjusting her pince-nez, which was tied to a tiny ivory button on her blouse, she murmured, "One day that bush is just green, and the next it's full of flowers. It's going to be spring." But it was still chilly outside and she was glad for the warmth of this musty old room that contained the precious past.

She looked around. The room was filled with colonial America (Vermont style), which meant not as much elegance as practicality. Black and brown were the dominant colors. Bits of gay pink and yellow woven into the rugs or chair bottoms of long ago had long since faded. Book spines, ridged or smooth, dusted silently away, the leather becoming like powder. On the pages, watery brown ink depicted life, the barest record of marrying, birthing, and dying. And all about the walls somber portraits of men and women measured the museum and their descendants.

Dorothy got up and walked through this room that had been her life for close to fifty years. She felt tears start. She was turning into a foolish old woman, she thought. Tears came easily to her now: not at all in keeping with the birdlike chirpiness she displayed for the occasional wanderer who happened across the little village. Turning her thoughts to the past week, she smiled. What a busy time it had been. Two, well, if you counted them all, three visitors in one week. And all interested in the Reverend Dean Irving Walker. First that lawyer fellow, then that good-looking gentleman with the goatee, and his pretty daughter with the spectacles. At least, she thought that was his daughter.

She opened the guest book and looked at the sign-ins: John Arnold, Newcastle; and right underneath, Beechmont, Newcastle, and Cynthia O'Rourke, Newcastle. Now here are three people, all from the same town, all interested in the same period of history, even the same individuals. They probably had never even met each other. Dorothy smiled mischievously and thought to herself, I'll just bet they'd like to meet each other. Why, when I mentioned Mr. Arnold to the other two they looked so surprised! Heavens! Why didn't I mention to that Beechmont gentleman that Mr. Arnold seemed terribly interested in him? I just forgot —my poor old brains get so rattled.

Opening the telephone book, she turned to the Yellow Pages, remembering that the young gentleman had mentioned he was a lawyer. She reached for the telephone, then stopped herself, saying, "Dotty Golightly, don't be an old busybody!" Then she giggled, "Oh, *do* be an old busybody." And she dialed the law firm's number.

A few hours after Dorothy's call John had rung Pica's Grill, and now he and Nick sat across from each other. Nick stared sullenly at the barrister.

"Nick, I'll come right to the point. How would you like to get your commercial pilot's license back?"

"You know I would."

"Now, you may not get back on the airlines, but I've got plenty of friends who might just be looking for a corporation pilot," continued John.

"Keep talking."

"It's not the best. I know you wanted to get back with United, but at least you'll be flying again."

"If I do what?"

"Nick, Nick, c'mon, we've been through a lot lately. Surely we can start trusting each other?"

"About the same time they close up the courthouse. What's the catch?"

"Nothing much, I just want you to arrange a little accident."

"Yeah, who do you want murdered?"

"Nick, you're spending too much time at Tony Pica's. That stuff will soften your brain."

"Baloney!"

"Listen, with this attitude—"

"Can the malarky. What's the job?" asked Nick.

"Do you know that local bum, Beechmont? You see him around mooching off the tourists."

"Yeah, I know him."

"Why don't you see if he'll just get himself ... ah, eliminated. He could fall into Beaver Creek. This would be a good time, as the spring runoff makes the water high," continued the lawyer.

"This got something to do with those royal land grants?"

John stared levelly at Nick, then said softly, "The less you know, the better."

Nick half rose in his chair, bitter words springing to his lips. But he sank back as John drove in for the final point. "Do this, and you'll be back flying in a month."

Nick said nothing.

"I take it by your silence that the answer is yes?"

Nick was thinking. Just as he had figured, the lawyer was crazy—and Nick was nuts to sit here listening to him.

There was no way he was going to hurt that old man. But he'd better be cool with this creep, just be cool.

"Then it's done. Now, leave. I've got plenty of work to do before the mayor's executive meeting."

As Nick closed the door behind him, John tented his fingers and gazed into the darkening room. He allowed himself a half-smile and thought that perhaps the end was in sight. Perhaps.

7 THE POLITICIANS

MERLE BAUMANN, an eighteen-year-old reporter for the *Newcastle Sentinel,* sat rapping out the latest disgruntled police officer's story. He flipped some chocolate drops into his mouth, and thought of city hall.

People reach a certain age and their brains must get stiff, he thought, like the police chief, and the mayor, and the aldermen. They really got corrupt with creeping age. The cops hated the chief, and the sewer workers hated the mayor, and lawyers hated the judges, and everybody hated the reporters. "Hey! That would make a great song," he said to no one in particular.

"Merle. Oh Merle. Let's wake up, Merle." It was Sarah Rice-Davis, the twenty-one-year-old city editor.

Merle sighed, and drawled an incomprehensible word that acknowledged the "Old Lady's" summons.

"The Gross One and His Gang are getting ready to go into secret session. Get over there, see what's going on. Give it the 'right-to-know' angle. And Merle, how about a little more anger in your tales of city hall? I'd hate to think you're getting mellow with age," she said.

Merle chuckled to himself, thinking, That Old Lady, mellowing out at eighteen. What a laugh. He reached for some old, wrinkled envelopes (for notes), and a chocolate bar, and went out of the newsroom into the night in his shirtsleeves.

At city hall all was noise and confusion. Two police officers stood at the mayor's office door, barring anyone not authorized to enter. This ban included the press, who milled about like disoriented puppies. Merle commenced scrawling, "Police State," and "Gestapo" (although he wasn't exactly sure what this latter word meant), on the backs of his wrinkled envelopes. Finally, sucking on his last chocolate-covered almond, he began to take notice of the people going in to the meeting. It looked like an executive council meeting. There was the mayor, with a cigar stuck in his moon face, and Council President R. Riley Ronk, whose eyes flicked like little whips at the crowd. Right behind them were Alderman Gino DeMattio and Alderman Roger D'Armour. Next came John Arnold, Newcastle's leading lawyer, carrying some kind of long, black box. Maybe he might be the one to approach, thought Merle. Maybe he could get a picture.

"Mr. Arnold, can I talk to you?"

John stopped momentarily, and looked at the boy coming toward him.

"Who are you?"

"Merle Baumann, reporter with the *Sentinel.* Like to ask you a few questions. What's going on? Like, why all the people?"

John stared at the young fellow, breathed "My God," and strode into the mayor's office. The door shut firmly behind him, and the two police officers stood in front, arms folded chest high, and glared at the throng.

"My God," Merle wrote on the back of a wrinkled envelope, and began to make up a news report in his head.

Parked outside, and just underneath the mayor's corner office, were three of the intrepid four and one diminutive electronics wizard. This latter individual occupied the whole back seat along with a tape recorder and other faintly sinister looking paraphernalia. A pair of headphones circled his blond head, and his fingers twiddled the dials in practiced rhythm. Pete O'Rourke was in his glory.

Crammed in the front were Ben, Cindy, and Nick, behind the wheel. Nick was speaking. "I've got to go in. The lawyer is expecting me. I don't know what's going to come out of this meeting. I do know that he's got the deeds and papers." He looked around, "By the way, where is Beechmont? Well, he's probably staying away. It's the best idea, what with all this." He tried to light a cigarette, but his hand shook so much that the match flickered out.

Cindy asked, "What's the matter Nick? You're shaking."

"Gees, I don't know, I feel like something's going to happen and I don't know what. You ever have that feeling?"

"Yeah, like just before a big test," Cindy said.

Nick glanced at Pete in the back seat and said, "How much does he know?"

"Not much," Ben said. "He's under pain of death to do what he's told and not to ask questions. Anyway, we bribed him with a soda."

"Some people come cheap," Nick said. He laughed mirthlessly. Then, without another word, he got out of the car and went into the building.

Cindy scrounged around so that she was facing the back seat and asked, "Are you picking up anything?"

But Pete, looking like Son of Space with his oversized headphones, just put a warning finger to his lips. Ben noticed that his eyes got wider and wider as he listened.

Outside, Newcastle went about its business in the warm May evening, oblivious to the events taking shape in the mayor's office.

"All right, gentlemen, please settle down. We've got some important matters to attend to," said Mayor Morse, looking around the long conference table.

R. Riley Ronk, president of the board of aldermen, took his gaze and held it. Ronk, who was almost as fat as the mayor, was, as Gordy Morse liked to describe him, "a health food nut." Because of his inclination to raw honey, sunflower seeds, and kelp, Ronk hated the mayor's cigars and candy bars. He was also after the mayor's job, feeling that once in, he could improve the health of Newcastleites just by power of example.

Alderman DeMattio, owner of the city's largest garbage disposal company, whose great clanking trucks had signs painted on them saying, "Beware—Bad Breath," was not after the mayor's job; he was after his head. This city father was adept at manipulating the *Newcastle Sentinel,* and was constantly blasting the mayor. It was rumored that DeMattio had "gone around the bend," and was receiving regular electroshock treatments.

Finally, Roger D'Armour: an impeccably dressed man, an individual who seemingly desired nothing and had no political ambitions. His district constantly reelected him (much to his embarrassment). He knew that all he really did at meetings of the city council was pull invisible skin off his nose, and murmur "Deary me" from time to time.

And down at the end of the table sat John Arnold, not attempting to hide his disgust at this group of political pariahs, the black box perched in front on him.

The mayor puffed on his cigar and wondered why he hadn't stayed in the shoe business with his brother. His gaze swept the room, and he noticed a little green device in one of the many potted plants hung all over the office. He squinted and read, "This Is A Bug," on the little sign. That must have been his wife's idea. He never knew when she was laughing at him. "This Is A Bug"—boy, the characters in this room right now are bugs, thought Gordy Morse.

"Gentlemen, I'll get right to business. I have decided to dispense with our regular agenda, at least right now, to take up a matter of grave importance," he began.

"Wait a minute. Hold on, yer honor," shrilled Gino DeMattio, jumping to his feet. "I object. We were supposed to come to a decision on the landfill." Then without pause, he turned to the others and began an oration. "I accuse the mayor of creating a health hazard, of playing fast and loose with the health of our children and our children's children. Furthermore—,"

"Gino, will you sit down? There ain't no reporters in here. I had 'em banned," said the mayor.

"—right to know, I accuse the mayor—"

"Gino, siddown and shut up!"

The alderman, mouth still open, sat down.

"Now, here's what's going on. You all know John Arnold down there." (All nodded in the lawyer's direction.) "Well, John brought me a piece of news the other day. It seems that he's found copies of an old land deed, and some sort of confession that says the city of Newcastle does not belong to us . . . uh, to the people. Uh, John, why don't you explain it?"

And with that Counselor Arnold opened the black box and unrolled Gideon's statement. As he read, heads leaned close. There were little murmurs and sighs as he read aloud old Templeton's suspicions of the murder of Jack Turner, and concluded with his own assessment of the situation: "The real danger to the status of the community is the fact of an heir. Since we know that the United States Government has, in fact, honored these grants, we will have those people involved. Not only that, if news of this got out, every nutcake from New Hampshire to California would be crowding into town claiming to be an heir. The federal courts would be tying our hands, and the business of the community *would be at a standstill.*"

As John continued to speak, the assembled men began to shift uncomfortably. They noticed that John's face had turned death-white and his eyes were like black holes; the contrast with his flaming red hair was appalling. Despite the warm night, the temperature in the room seemed to drop.

Alderman DeMattio said, "It's a plot, a plot by you, Gordon Morse, to make money, to try some trick."

"Come off it, Gino," said Ronk, speaking for the first time. "I think this is a helluva story; someone ought to make a movie out of it. Y'know, they lived naturally in those days, no chemicals or additives in the food." He nervously cracked a sunflower seed between his teeth.

Alderman D'Armour nearly rubbed his nose raw in agitation, and was heard to say "Tsk, tsk" at least ten times. He wondered why nobody asked about the original grant. Well, he wasn't going to bring it up if no one else did.

Mayor Morse was busy trying to find a Milky Way in his desk drawer.

All were terrified, but trying not to show it. The room felt freezing cold and even the lights seemed dim. Their eyes were riveted on John's face. Its paleness glowed with a greenish light, and his eyes were like fiery coals.

"Fools," he thundered. "Fools!" The officials froze. "You've got to decide—start doing your duty, for the first time in your meaningless lives!"

"Now hold on, John," began Alderman DeMattio, his voice trembling.

"Don't tell me to hold on, and don't you dare call me by my first name!" John's fury was a palpable thing. The city fathers were frozen in fear.

It was the mayor who broke the spell. "All right, all right, get rid of the papers. Burn 'em up, just burn 'em up."

And light returned to the room, along with the warm air of May, and the office once again smelled of Mrs. Morse's potted plants. The aldermen looked around and blinked, as if awaking from a bad dream.

"Th-th-that sounds g-g-good, except supposing there's one of these heirs around?" offered Alderman D'Armour nervously.

The mayor looked at John and asked, "Are there any around, near as you can figure out?"

John looked at the aldermen, thinking, There's not one here I could trust, nor would I want to. He lied, "No, there's none around."

"Well, I vote we burn the damn things, although that document is awfully pretty," said Ronk. "All those in favor?"

"Aye."

"Aye."

"Aye."

"Aye."

"Good," said Mayor Morse, directing his remarks to John. "You heard the vote; will you take care of it?"

John's face had regained its former color, and he nodded in assent.

Then, once again, the mayor's attitude was one of dismissal. John picked up the box and went out of the office.

In the corridor a television news setup was in progress. The announcer, an older man of twenty-five with a wispy black mustache, was speaking directly into a 1935-style, automatic movie camera on a wooden tripod. "And once again the executive council of the city of Newcastle has reverted to a police state, and barred the press and the public by going into secret session."

Pausing, he went to the camera, made an adjustment, started it up, let it run, and stepped into camera range. "As you can see, two burly police officers are blocking the way. This appears to be in direct violation of the state's 'right-to-know' law. Most certainly the governor will be informed, the federal authorities. Mayor Morse is in for it this time."

John looked around, spotted Nick, and steered him into the men's room. Once in, he looked under the stalls for feet. Satisfied that no one else was there, he turned to the ex-football player and asked, "Did you do the job?"

"Uh, no, I can't find the old geezer. He's up and disappeared." Nick hoped the lie would work.

John's face darkened.

"Did you try? Where is he? It's got to be done!" the lawyer said.

"I'll keep looking. Y'know the creek's been awful swift these past weeks. He's an old drunk—maybe he fell in!"

John glared at him. He was sure Nick was lying. They

all were lying to him. He wouldn't trust a mother's son of them, ever again. He clutched the long, ornate box, and bumped out through the men's room door.

Meanwhile, down in Nick's car, Pete was pushing buttons and switches that caused the tape to rewind with a whirr and plastic *snick-snick*. Pete loved these little noises, and the black and red switches, winking lights, alligator clips, and rainbows of wires that made up his electrical kingdom. But he, being eleven, was also nosy. He spoke to the conspirators in the front seat: "What's goin' on? What's royal grants, and how come those jerks want to burn them? An' how come—"

Upon hearing Pete's piping voice, shrill in its curiosity, Ben closed his eyes tight and summoned up awesome fantasies: the great and terrible Thor, the wily and evil Fu Manchu, the gross and greedy Godzilla, the raging and raucous Rodan, and the heinous and horrible Hulk. Armed with the sheer might of these powerful figures, he directed a glare of such malevolence at the quailing Peter that this worthy shrunk to a mite and was silent. To further seal his lips, his sister promised punishments of such dire consequence as to do in the child, at least temporarily.

Ben said, "OK, give me the tape (which the Whiz Kid yielded up meekly). Now, I think we better get out of here and go see Beechmont."

And packing up the gear, they left Nick's car and headed up the street.

That night, as clouds scudded across a gibbous moon, a bulky figure tinkered with the trade-entrance door to a downtown Newcastle office building. Suddenly the door opened, and the figure quietly crept up the fire stairs until he came to the sixth floor. Placing a tool bag and a pry-bar on the floor, he knelt by a partially glass office door. Lights shining up from the street below brought the letters on the door into bold relief. They read, "Arnold, Leggett, Primrose, and Bourne."

June was under way in Newcastle. There was that day when all awoke and behold! A richness of green spread and curled over the hills and fields, around the homes, and wrapped the trees—infinite green: pale, deep, sea, aqua, Lincoln, pea, forest, and so forth. Sweet warmth abounded, all the sweeter for its emergence from the sere and ghostly winter.

But Nick was missing, and it was hard to tell who missed him most.

Was it John, whose office had been broken into, the safe cracked and only one thing taken—the box, the fancy, long box that held the key to Newcastle's fate? Or was it the brave group of friends, threatened by known—and perhaps unknown—powers, who through both fair and underhanded endeavor sought the truth, sought to solve the riddle of Newcastle? Perhaps it was the bartender at Tony Pica's, who, while wiping the sticky counter at 8:00 A.M., would gaze out the big plate-glass window, half expecting the bulky shape to come bumping in the door. Or did Old Burgoyne miss him most? After all, it was the great gray cat with the golden eyes that first had seen the good in Nick. Anyway, he was missed.

Beechmont, Cindy, and Ben sat in Beechmont's cabin and wondered aloud, "Where is Nick?"

"Near as I can piece out," said Beechmont, "he went into city hall and hasn't been seen since."

Cindy, busily wiping her glasses, began talking to herself.

Ben got sarcastic. "How about letting us know the workings of your mighty brain?"

"I think I have it," exclaimed Cindy. "Now, Nick was in the car with us, acting kinda funny. He shook so. He said he felt like something was going to happen. We do know that Mr. Arnold had the original documents. Now, it looks like the city fathers have decided to destroy the papers, and gave Lawyer Arnold the job, and probably he put them in his office safe—"

"And Nick broke in and got 'em. You don't suppose he's going to try to sell them to the highest bidder?" interjected Ben.

Beechmont leaned back, puffing on his pipe, and said, "At least the authentic royal deed is safe."

"Yeah, but where is it? I didn't notice it around here," Cindy said.

"It's in the best place ever—hangin' up in the Wheeler Room at the library. They were glad to get an old-time Vermont sampler to pretty up the place," said Beechmont.

Ben chimed in, "We're noplace, 'cause Nick has the proof, and all we have is the grant and what we've figured out, plus those copies of Miz Templeton's." He hit the floor with his fist in disgust.

Cindy had the strangest feeling that she wanted to put her arm around him. "What can we do?" she asked, looking up.

"Wal, it appears that there ain't a whole heckuva hang we kin do about it, 'cept wait, mebbe," replied Beechmont. He looked at the two youngsters with a hint of sadness. It wouldn't do right now to tell them of his proof of the rock carvings and the bones. He would keep that to himself, at least for the time being.

And so they sat, while Burgoyne yawned and stretched and shed, as it was the beginning of summer.

John Arnold was furious, with an anger that was making him nauseous. Victory had been within his grasp, but then the Templeton testament had been stolen and now that stupid fool, Nick Tomasi, had disappeared. No doubt the two disappearances were connected, he mused bitterly. He wondered when he'd get the blackmail note from Nick. The lawyer's spies and inquiries had availed nothing. He thought of the old lady, Mrs. Golightly, calling him about Beechmont's visit.

John sat in his swivel chair and twisted and turned, rolling from the desk to the window and back. At one point he stopped at the window and looked down. There, way below, were the usual late afternoon strollers. But wait, he noticed one with white hair and a little beard. John couldn't recognize the face, but it put him in mind again of —Beechmont!

And then he felt as if some ancient hand were pushing him. The old fury rose again. There he was, the heir apparent. The owner of John Arnold's town. An old drunk heir, unworthy of even mowing the grass in Partridge Street Park. John swung his chair in little tight arcs, his fist tightening on the daggerlike letter opener.

That night it turned cooler, causing a mist to rise from the creek. Beechmont was alone in his cabin. He had arranged the bones of his ancestor so that, except for a few missing here and there, he had the entire skeleton of a full-grown man. He had been a short man, with heavy hands and leg bones that looked like they had been broken and healed. A rugged old scout. Now Beechmont gazed on them lovingly. He was thinking that all he really wanted out of all this was a decent burial for the captain here, and perhaps a pension from the city. Heck, he'd deed the place back to the people of Newcastle. All he needed was a bit of money to fix up this old cabin. What he'd really like to do was write a history of Newcastle. Maybe the city would give him an office. It didn't hurt to daydream, he thought.

Beechmont was humming to himself and brushing the dug-up bones when he heard a *whump* against the side of the building. Turning, he watched fascinated and transfixed as a small, glowing hole at the base of the wall suddenly burst into a sheet of flames. Tearing himself away from the table of bones, he reached the door and began struggling to open it.

It was barred, and he was trapped. His eyes widened in terror as fingers of flames crawled across the ceiling and dropped like little bits of bright paint over the table, stove, and bookcases.

Far down the creek bank a red-haired, white-faced man stumbled, the puckerbrush tearing at his clothes, his hands reeking of gasoline. Crazily he would stop and plunge them into the creek, each hand scrabbling at the other like a claw. Then he'd run and stumble some more, his shoes filling with water. Once he turned, hearing a loud *whoosh,* and saw the creek and the underbrush light up like day as the cabin turned into a mighty torch, flaring into the sky.

The next morning, little curls of smoke eddied up into the warm air as the State Police Criminal Investigation Division combed the gray ashes of the cabin for clues. Little knots of people stood around, talking in low tones. Walking back and forth between ashes and people was Police Chief Dennis Slocum, his tired eyes looking like they'd seen one too many fires, one too many beaten wives, and one too many mangled, car-wrecked bodies.

One of the CID men spoke to the chief. "It looks like whoever lived here never got out. Looks to have been sleeping. The bones are burnt clean. By the way, who did live here?"

Denny Slocum rubbed the bridge of his nose with thumb and forefinger and said, "Just an old-timer named Beechmont. Not a bad old guy—been around for years."

"Oh, OK. We'll get a report to you in a few days, Chief."

Ben and Cindy also stood near the cabin's ashes, holding hands tightly and crying quietly.

Cindy choked, "Oh Ben, he was the best friend I had in all the world."

"Yeah," said Ben, wiping his eyes on his sleeve, "he was a good old soak, I mean, guy. Well, maybe we ought to go home. C'mon Burgoyne," he called.

The cat was prancing around the fire site like a kitten, batting at bugs and butterflies, playful as you please.

Ben regarded him sternly. "C'mon, old cat, don't you think you can act sad? After all, the old man was your friend too!" But Burgoyne simply padded over to them, rubbed up against their legs, purred, and twitched his whiskers.

Evidently the late Beechmont had kept up his dues to the American Legion, so the bones found at the burned-out cabin were buried in Pine Wood Cemetery with full military honors. Every time the honor guard, snappy in white gloves, fittings, and legionnaire's blue, fired off a ceremonial round over the grave, Ben felt like a blow had been struck in his heart.

Only a few people had attended the small graveside service. Cindy and Ben were there, of course, as were Ben's mother, and the entire O'Rourke clan. The O'Rourkes were very respectful of mourning and were present at many wakes and funerals. Chief Slocum was there too. He had had to arrest Beechmont on many occasions for being drunk in public (most of the time to save him from passing out in a snowbank), and they had become friends. In fact, when Beechmont was ready to be arrested, he'd always insisted on being arrested by the chief. Dennis Slocum had seen that lately Beechmont had quit drinking, and he was grateful for this, yet he often missed their old relationship. The bartender and a few regulars of Pica's Grill came, but they stayed off by themselves, as if belonging to a slightly different tribe. Even one of the characters who hung around *behind* Pica's Grill was there, but he stood very far away. One would never know whether this citizen had come out of genuine grief for Beechmont or concern over the half gallon of muscatel he had hidden in the old Templeton crypt.

And then it was over, and all drifted away under one of those rare cloudless days of late spring. That left only the gravediggers, who quickly began shoveling dirt into the open grave.

Later, after supper, when a gentle, balmy eventide had settled over Newcastle, Cindy and Ben sat on the front step of O'Rourke's Fine Foods. They talked in low, almost reverential tones.

"Y'know, I liked old Beechmont a lot, and . . ." Ben's voice trailed off.

"I know it's hard to talk about. It's funny, I'm sad that he's gone, but I don't feel bad. I mean, I feel bad that he's gone, but I *don't* feel bad. Do you know what I'm talking about?" Cindy asked.

"Yeah, kinda. It's being all scary-like inside, but it's not a bad scary, it's, well, a good scary," said Ben as he scratched with a stick on the sidewalk.

"And look at Burgoyne; he's on top of the world," said Cindy, pausing. "Listen, we should decide what to do next. Beechmont would want us to do something."

"So what do we do with both Beechmont and Nick gone?" Ben asked gloomily. "All our papers were burned up in the fire. I mean, what do we have? And what about that fire? I noticed Beechmont was always very careful about his pipe ashes, and at this time of year he certainly wasn't using his woodstove—looks suspicious to me."

"But only we knew how careful Beechmont was, and that he had stopped drinking wine. The so-called official investigation said he was smoking in bed," replied Cindy. She paused, as if in thought, then she said, "Well, at least we still have the tape recording."

"Oh, my God, what about the bug!" Ben interrupted.

"It's OK. My brother's class had their annual tour of city hall yesterday and he managed to sneak it out while they were in the mayor's office.

"That's a relief. So what we're left with is a tape recording, and that's it, " said Ben, glancing at Cindy. "You thinking what I'm thinking?"

"That this fire was no accident?" Cindy queried.

And Ben took it up, "I'll bet that lawyer, Arnold, knows all about this."

"You don't suppose *he* set fire to Beechmont's cabin?" Cindy asked.

They stared at each other as the street lights of Newcastle went on in the balmy dark. And now the scared feeling was all bad.

It was late spring in Newcastle, and the friendly Vermont skies were sending down torrents of rain. Students slipped and splashed up and down the broad stone stairs of the high school. The crowd included Cindy O'Rourke, the usual stack of books clutched in her arms. Just as she entered the building, she heard an announcement over the public address system summoning her to the office. Feeling a little jab of fear, she went in.

Old Mrs. Dooley called her over to the high counter, "Cynthia, Cynthia, there is a letter here for you. And we would appreciate it if you would not think of this office as your personal post office." Mrs. Dooley pursed her thin lips and sniffed as she proffered a cheap white envelope.

Taking the letter, Cindy dashed out of the office to her locker. There she examined it. The envelope was smudged, and the postmark read, "Granville, N.Y." The address just said "Cindy O'Rourke, Newcastle High, Newcastle, Vt." There wasn't even a ZIP code on it. And suddenly Cindy felt all warm and shivery. It was a little like the feeling she had at night, in her room, when she thought about boys— Ben mostly.

Opening the letter, she read:

Dear Cindy,

Don't be scared, but this letter is from your old pal, Beechmont. Yep, I didn't die in the fire, but I figured I'd better get out of town for a while.

Nick is with me, and he's got those items we were all so interested in. Nick says to be careful of you-know-who.

I say don't lose hope, everything's going to be OK. Tell Ben howdy, and both of you be careful and keep your ears peeled. Don't do anything until you hear from us.

Your Pal,
Beechmont Turner Walker

Cindy held the letter to her, whispering, "He's alive! He's alive! He's alive! Thanks, God. Thanks, God." She had to find Ben to tell him the good news. Cindy did a little dance right there in the hall with somber, rain-soaked students stomping all around her.

8 THE FIRE

WHEN BEECHMONT RUSHED to the door of his cabin while the walls leapt and crawled in yellow flames, he found it barred. There was no escape, and he knew his time had come. Yet, stumbling away in blind panic, his clothes already smoldering, he spotted the window, and without thinking he ran for it and flung himself against the glass. Amazingly the glass and frames shattered easily, and before he knew it he was outside the house, scrabbling on the wet ground on his hands and knees. Gaining his feet, he ran in fear, gasping, until he reached the creek and fell in. The water quenched his smoking clothes, and as he crawled up the opposite bank of the creek, he realized his body hadn't been singed at all. He lay there, exhausted and trembling, until he heard the sirens. Peeking through the underbrush, he saw his beloved cabin turned into a giant blaze as the fire trucks circled, and firemen jumped and scurried around it. It was no use, no use at all, and the roof and walls collapsed in fiery glory, the flames and floating hot red ashes making an aura in the night.

Beechmont sat spread-legged on a muddy bank, and tears struggled into his eyes. He wiped them and sniffed for what seemed like hours.

When dawn came, he was dry eyed, but there was a weight on his chest. He felt like he wanted to drink, and might have if a jug had been handy. Hell, he had even lost his favorite pipe in the fire.

Taking another look at the cabin (which was by now a heap of ashes with only the sturdy iron railroad stove standing, twisted and black, in the middle), he saw Denny Slocum talking to some tough-looking men and a couple of state troopers. And he spotted—yes, it was them—Ben and Cindy. They looked like they were holding on to each other. The big gray cat was with them.

Beechmont was on the verge of running back and hollering, "Hey, I'm all right! I ain't dead!" when he stopped. Maybe he'd better just disappear for a while, he thought. He suspected that the lawyer had set the fire, and he didn't want to draw Arnold's attention back to the kids. Even worse, maybe Nick had turned coats again and set the blaze himself. Booze could make a man do almost anything, he knew.

Then he remembered the bones, the remains of his ancestor. By God, they'd probably think that old skeleton was him! And the Legion would bury "Beechmont" with military honors—taps and rifles, which was what he had always wanted.

He looked again at the kids. They looked so small and alone. He wanted to run over and hug the both of them. But he had to have time to think, and he knew that he was doing the right thing by staying out of sight. "Goodbye, Ben and Cindy. Goodbye for a while," he said softly, and then turned and headed for the railroad tracks.

Hiking along the tracks, skipping the ties and gandy-dancing the rails, Beechmont felt young, like when he'd hoboed around the country years before. The Fair would come to Newcastle, and he would skedaddle with the carnival—King Teet's Games and Shows. It had been fun, and good money too—long summer days lying out back of the cook tent, drinking sweet wine and smoking "Bugler." He remembered the smell of summer grass and dusty streets in New England towns. After the tents were up, he'd drift into town in that warm, misty dawn known only to hoboes, golfers, and horse players, and look for the early opening saloon. The first cold beer of the day would be God's gift, cutting the throat muck of last night's wine. That old familiar barroom stink, like the delicate fragrance of a woman once loved, was never forgotten.

Voices off to one side of the tracks brought him out of his reverie. Could it be a hobo jungle in this day and age? Old instincts warned him to approach silently. Creeping up to a small clearing, Beechmont pushed aside some branches and peered in. There, sitting on the ornate long box containing the papers and parchments that had led to murder, attempted murder, chicanery, and all kinds of foul deeds, was Nick Tomasi. He was dressed in his sport jacket, tie, and snap-brim hat, and looked a little like Clark Gable stuck on the road in that old movie *It Happened One Night*. He was passing a bottle of "Sneaky Pete" to a couple of knights of the road. "Oh, my God, he's back drinking," muttered Beechmont. But when the bottle circulated back to the big ex-football hero, he refused his rightful swallow.

Seeing that things were safe, Beechmont stepped into the clearing. "Hello, Nick."

The man addressed looked up with a face that slowly drained of color. Around him, like startled courtiers, the ragged band of tramps stared at the intruder.

"What's the matter, Nick, cat et yer tongue?"

Nick scrambled to his feet. "W·W·Wha—. You're sup·posed to be dead!"

"Wal, I ain't. Leastwise this don't look like heaven, more like hell. (Sorry, boys.) Perhaps that's where I'll wind up anyway," Beechmont said.

"But you're dead—it said so on the car radio."

"Listen, if you pinch me and I holler, will ya believe I'm alive?"

"OK, OK, I believe it," said Nick, his face beginning to lose its ashen hue.

"Good. Now, we gotta talk."

"Sure. Here, boys, finish her off. There's another in that bag."

"Thanks, Nick."

"Yer a good fellow, Nick."

"We won't fergit ya, Nick."

The two men started walking through the underbrush toward the narrow logging road that paralleled the tracks. Nick clutched the long black box as if his life was contained therein. They walked in silence until they reached Nick's beat·up Chevy.

"Beechmont, how did you get out of the fire? The radio said they found your bones. It looked like you'd been sleeping."

"I'll tell you about it later," Beechmont said, looking at the younger man. Nick looked distraught. His white shirt was dirty, and his clothes looked like they hadn't left his body in a week. His breath was foul, but not boozy, and his swarthy cheeks were covered with black stubble. Beech·mont took a deep breath and asked, "Nick, did you fire my cabin?"

There was a deathly stillness; not even the sound of

spring birds twittering in the soft air could be heard. The two men were frozen in time, confronting each other.

"No, honest to God, Beechmont," Nick said hoarsely. He felt his eyes burn and grow wet. He'd been doing a lot of crying lately, he thought.

Beechmont noticed the tears. "That's good enough for me."

They both relaxed, and Nick put the box in his car trunk.

"What next?" asked Beechmont.

"I don't know about you," Nick said, "but I'm taking off. I'm going to find a good lawyer, tell him the whole story, and milk that S.O.B. Arnold and the whole damn town dry!"

Beechmont walked around in a little circle as Nick went on, his voice getting more and more excited: "You come along. In fact, this makes it perfect, you being the heir." When Beechmont remained silent, kicking at pebbles and twigs in the road, Nick added, "And don't worry about money, the lawyer paid me well. Think of it, you and me, we'll be sitting pretty."

Finally Beechmont spoke. "Ain't you fergettin' something?"

"What? Oh, you mean the kids. Well, they'll be all right."

"Is that so? Listen, Nick, the way I figger it, John Arnold tried to kill me."

"So, you're thinking he'll hurt the kids. Well, don't worry, he told me himself he wasn't interested in them."

"That was before you took off with the box, and before he burned my cabin."

"Yeah, I guess so," said Nick, rubbing his bristly chin.

"And you told us yourself that he's crazy—his face turning dead white and all. Be honest, Nick. Is there any reason why he wouldn't take out after those kids?"

"But—"

"But me no buts. Those kids are all alone in Newcastle."

Nick began to twist around in frustration. Arguments swelled up and died as he envisioned Cindy's face, her big glasses, and her way of wrinkling her nose; Ben, his way of looking earnest; that cat, Burgoyne, the first one who trusted him. And they had never paid him anything, they just plain trusted him.

Beechmont was looking at him, head cocked. He knew enough to be still when a man was making up his mind.

"OK, OK, old man, you win. But first, let's stay out of town for a little while. I have a widowed sister in Granville. She can put us up. For chrissake, look at you! You look like you could use a bath, and I must smell like a billy goat."

"Sounds good, Nick, but I'll want to contact the kids as soon as we get there."

"Yeah, but if you call 'em at home, their folks'll get suspicious. Pretty soon it'll be all over town that you're still alive. Better that you're dead, for a while. That might keep Arnold quiet for the time being."

"You've got a point, but I hope those kids will be careful," said Beechmont.

"Hey, Ben's a sharp one, and Cindy's no slouch. They'll look after themselves 'til we get back," Nick assured him.

"Then there's nothing left to do but to get to your sister's." Beechmont suddenly felt very tired, dirty, and hungry. And off they drove in Nick's car through the new green trees.

Back in the clearing, the hoboes were cracking the new

bottle of muscatel. They were pleasantly loaded, and all around birds squeaked and called a spring song of joy.

Meanwhile, attorney John Arnold had taken to prowling the streets of Newcastle late at night. He could not explain this behavior to himself, but he felt enormously protective of the city now that he had gotten rid of the usurper, that descendant of Scouter Jack Turner. John knew he had repulsed an invader. He saw himself as a feudal lord who had won a mighty victory over marauders, and saved his village. His village by right of descent.

He had become increasingly haggard, his flaming red hair even more brilliant as contrasted to his white face. His manner had become threatening, so much so that his few friends had avoided him. And he had all but ceased his law practice. Chief Slocum and the Newcastle Police had become used to seeing his gaunt frame wandering through the streets and alleys, looking over his shoulder from time to time, glaring fiercely at late-night passersby. Denny Slocum's private opinion of lawyers was not high, and John's behavior confirmed it for him.

One misty Friday night, John stood on the corner of Emporium Avenue and Central Row. He was muttering under his breath: "The flames, the flames. It's done, I did it, and never, never can they take this town from me. I'm right, right as rain. Good there was no rain that night. A fire bomb, that's what did it. Oh, they'll never know. Boy, I feel hot, hot and cold and shuddery. Where's Nick? He's gone. I trusted him, and he's gone. I'll kill him and burn the papers. I'll kill everyone. Oh my belly hurts. Oh dear, oh dear! If I bite my fingers. Those kids! They know, they know. They're next. What's that, what's that you say? Oh,

I see, there's no one there. I'd better walk, walk around. The police will arrest me, for I know the law. I am the lawyer. I'll just wipe my eyes because I am the lawyer." And he walked up Central Row in the street-lit night, clasping and unclasping his hands behind his back, his mouth moving imperceptibly, his head shaking.

It was almost time to plant tomatoes, which meant that Memorial Day would soon be here in all its blue, green, and sunlit glory. Dorothy Golightly opined that the good Lord loved Vermont a little, but more on Memorial Day, for he always sent a good one.

Michael O'Rourke, who closed his store only at night and on Sunday, was busily laying out seedlings and tomato plants in front of O'Rourke's Fine Foods. He stopped in his labors and stretched. The sun felt good. Soon he'd be rolling the awning down. B'Jee, warm weather feels good, he thought. How in hell do we survive the winters around here?

Ben Weisman had tried out for the Newcastle High baseball team and made it. He found he was a natural first baseman. His increasingly lanky frame made it easy to glove the sometimes wild throws of the team's shortstop. He was getting better at the plate, and he'd make the varsity for sure next year.

Cindy had been up to her ears in spring concerts and orchestra practices. Her classmates had laughed at her, picking the tuba as her instrument. But, since no one else wanted it, her choice earned her a place on the school band.

And now both kids were studying for exams and feeling a gut-tightening fear at the thought of the little blue exam books, of the absolute silence in each exam room and of the horrible sensation that they simply knew nothing, absolutely nothing about anything and that the exam books would stay blank, or get blanker.

So in the rush of the end of school, the events of winter were pushed aside. Tomato plants were put in with care as people in gardens, on their knees, looked to heaven to send them no more frosts. The fishing season, already two months old, was in full swing. The lakes and streams, so quiet and cold in winter, now filled with boats, waders, and the faint whir of a good cast. Scores of elementary school kids had trooped to Washington, D.C., to view the monuments, sleep four to a room, and remember only the swan boats on the Potomac River's Tidal Basin when they returned. Boats were caulked, sanded, painted, and put on their moorings. Lake cabins were opened and aired. Office workers rushed to sign up for their vacations, hoping that someone else had not picked the choice times. And everyone anticipated Newcastle's biggest blowout of the year: opening on the Fourth of July (as it had for 148 years) was the "stupendous, extraordinary, colossal, incredible, sensational, titanic, Newcastle Fair."

As Memorial Day began the work of summer, so the Fourth (as celebrated at the Newcastle Fair) would begin the fun of summer.

9 THE FAIR

IT WAS THE FINAL WEEK of school; that half-sleepy, half-exciting time when very little held your interest and dozing was overlooked. In one ground-floor classroom, the entire class slipped through a window as the teacher droned on and on.

At noon one day, Ben and Cindy sat under an elm tree at the far end of the athletic field, sharing their lunches.

They had become very conscious of each other this spring. Ben, when he looked at Cindy—at the way her big glasses slipped down on her nose, and the softness of her long brown hair—felt warm and kind of shaky inside. Sometimes it was like before a baseball game, or before he got up to bat—an excitement around his heart. Only this feeling was better. Cindy, on her part, had never quite realized how handsome Ben was—that is, until recently. She'd look at him, and wow! Her feelings made her blink her eyes.

"Cindy, I got a bologna sandwich here—ya want it?"

"Yuck, that is the most nutritionally unsound sandwich I have ever heard of. Here, eat this Twinkie and be nourished!"

Ben took a swig of milk, leaned against the tree, and asked, "So, where d'ya think old Beechmont is now?"

"You know as much about it as I do. All I know is what was in the note. I don't know when he's coming back, or if he's coming back," said Cindy. She paused and bit her lower lip. "'Course you heard about that lawyer, John Arnold."

"No, what's he been up to?"

"I heard Chief Slocum talking to my father, and he told him that Mr. Arnold is walking around town late at night talking to himself. Acting nuttier than a fruitcake. Or maybe it was fruitier than a nutcake!" She giggled.

But Ben looked serious and said that it wasn't funny, pointing out that the lawyer was still dangerous, and they'd better do like Beechmont said: take care of themselves.

Meanwhile, a few days later in the school office, Mrs. Dooley held another letter in her hand and tapped it on the counter. She was contemplating throwing it away: That Cynthia O'Rourke. More personal mail. Oh well, school's almost done. I'll give it to her. But she shouldn't be using the school's office as her personal post office.

Ben was walking home from the last baseball practice, but his mind wasn't on first base. More than likely it was out in left field. So this is love, and it's Cindy, and, oh boy, what a feeling, he thought. Ben's head was in the clouds as he strolled under the leafy trees, and he didn't hear the car as it screeched around the corner and headed right for him.

Afterward he remembered a long, screaming yowl like cats make when they are mating. It woke him up just in time for him to leap out of the way of the onrushing car. Scrambling up from the sidewalk, trembling in every part of his body, he looked after the car as it careened down the street. He thought he caught a flash of red hair, but couldn't be sure. He was still shaking when he let himself into the apartment.

The telephone was ringing as he got in and he jumped for it.

"Ben, it's Cindy."

"Yes. Hi, Cindy."

"Listen, I have a letter from Beechmont. He and Nick are coming back soon. We're to meet them at a place by the railroad tracks."

"Oh, good. That's good," Ben said, unable to keep the quaver out of his voice.

"What's the matter? You sound funny."

"It's nothing. I . . . uh . . . almost got run over by a car. I guess I'm still shook up."

"Oh God! Are you all right? I'm coming right over!"

"No. I'm OK, I'm OK."

"Oh, Ben. I love you, Ben. If something had happened to you—"

"Cindy, I·I·I·I love . . . you . . . too," Ben said, feeling his eyes get wet. "Cindy?"

"Yes?"

"How come we're shouting at each other?"

The day of the reunion of the band of four was cloudy and cool. In his letter to Cindy Beechmont had drawn a crude map showing a clearing by the railroad tracks, across Beaver Creek. This would be the meeting place.

Ben and Cindy were on their way to the rendezvous.

After finally declaring their love for each other they had become shy, touching fingertips now and again, but mostly being respectful of one another. When their eyes met, they blushed and glanced away. They knew great joy and great agony, and the usually talkative pair became tongue-tied with each other.

Padding majestically along with them, sleek in his new summer coat, was Old Burgoyne. Since the adventure had begun, this cat had given a full measure of devotion to his human charges. Now he walked like a guard, somewhat away from the kids, pausing occasionally to contemplate them, paw upraised.

Reaching the clearing, they looked around. It obvious-ly had been recently evacuated. Ashes from a cookfire were still warm, and empty wine bottles were strewn about. There was no one else there yet.

"We'd better wait for a while," said Cindy.

"Yeah." There was a long silence, punctuated by the singing katydids.

They were very conscious of each other, alone, out in the woods. The air was soft and smelled sweet, and every now and then a bird took off in lofty song. Cindy glanced at Ben, so cute and serious, and suddenly he turned and looked into her eyes. In a moment, they were in each other's arms. He leaned his head toward hers and kissed her full on the lips.

"Cindy." Ben's voice was almost choking.

"Yes, Ben." She ducked her head shyly so that her glasses slipped down on her nose.

"I-I-I-I-I . . . oh nuts . . . it's hard to say. What's—" his voice trailed off.

"Yeah, it sure is. Hey," Cindy looked up, her eyes shin-ing, "let's not say anything—I mean, let's just take things easy for a while."

The relief on Ben's face was obvious. "That's a good idea. After all, we . . . oh." He struggled for control of his universe, picking up twigs, cracking them, and throwing them into the underbrush.

Cindy looked around. "I wonder what's keeping Beechmont and Nick?"

"Right behind you, honey." And there was Beechmont, looking fit and smiling broadly, his beard trimmed.

Cindy flung herself into his arms, saying, "Oh, Beechmont, you're alive. You're alive!"

"Yep, honey. Take more than a shyster lawyer to put me under," he answered, hugging her and patting her shoulder. Then he reached out with his free hand to Ben. "Howdy boy. Have you been takin' care of my little girl?"

Ben shook Beechmont's hand, his smile showing his pleasure at seeing the tough old man.

There was a rustling in the bushes, and Nick Tomasi shouldered into the clearing, carrying the black metal box. They greeted him and settled themselves in a circle. Cindy looked around and exclaimed, "Thank God we're all here and safe." She hugged her knees.

Ben was itching with curiosity. "Beechmont, how did you escape the fire? I mean, whose bones were those they found, and how—"

"Whoa there. Let me tell you what happened." And after filling and lighting his pipe, he told the kids (and a wide-eyed Burgoyne) of his discoveries at Mead's Rock, the bones of his ancestor, and the rest. He finished, "And so old Jack Turner got a military funeral at last. Only thing is, he's got my name on the gravestone 'steada his'n."

The whole story had now come together in Cindy's mind: the adventures of Scouter Jack Turner, his royal grant and settling along the Beaver Creek; John Arnold's fury; Kohega's terrifying flight with the baby; the Reverend

Dean Irving Walker's loving shelter; and Arnold's name-sake's efforts to keep the truth from being known. She spoke up: "We have to let everyone know. I mean, it's the only way."

"I agree, Cindy, but how?" asked Beechmont.

"How about taking the whole thing to the newspaper?" she suggested.

"No, those youngsters are too busy battling city hall. They'd probably use it as a weapon. That's not what we want," Beechmont said.

"And obviously we can't go to the town fathers. Hell, they think the documents are burned up anyway," said Nick gloomily, lighting a cigarette. "No, we have to get the message directly to the people themselves."

"Yer right, but how?" asked Beechmont again. "I don't suppose there's any one place that everybody's together at one time?"

Cindy was lost in thought. She barely murmured, "Newcastle Fair."

"What was that?" Beechmont glanced at her quickly.

"Newcastle Fair. The whole town's there on Independence Day," she said.

"By God, yer right. We can tell them then. Let me think," Beechmont said. He sucked furiously at his pipe. "OK, now here's what we're going to do."

They leaned their heads together as they plotted. A half hour went by. It was quiet, except for the low murmur of their voices.

Suddenly, there were cracking gunshots, and bullets snicked through the leaves. Nick rose like an avenging line-backer, enveloped the other three in his big arms, and the whole gang fell flat on the ground. "Lie quiet," he growled.

It was quiet once again. Finally Nick looked up and said, "I guess the coast is clear."

They got up one by one, examining themselves for injuries.

"That settles it," Beechmont said breathlessly. "We have to stick together until this is all done. But Newcastle ain't the safest place to be right now."

"Well," said Nick, "it's back to my sister's. She'll be glad to let you all stay for a few days. She lives about thirty miles from here."

Ben frowned. "Hold on. Cindy and I can't just take off. What about our folks?"

Beechmont said, "Yer right, but I'm scared that red-headed John is really after you two kids, as well as me and Nick; them shots were intended for all of us."

"It's only going to be a few days. The fair is next weekend. But we have to make sure our folks know," Cindy pointed out.

"You can call them from my sister's."

Off they went to Nick's car, the two kids trailing slowly, all the joy drained out, for now they were just plain scared.

Helen O'Rourke went from chair to chair: she couldn't sit still. "Oh, my God, where are they? It's been a whole day and no word," she moaned, as she wrung her hands.

"Honey, try to relax. Denny Slocum has the whole force looking for them. They'll be found." Mike O'Rourke reached over and patted his wife's shoulder.

"Deborah, where could they be?" Helen wept openly.

Some of the new-found confidence that Deborah Weisman had gathered was leaking away, and she had reverted to biting her nails. "I don't know, I just don't know. Ben went out, said he was coming over here, and ... he was gone." Deborah dabbed at her eyes.

Mike blundered in, "You don't suppose they ran off and got married?"

"Oh, dear God, *no.*" Both women reached to each other for comfort. Then the telephone rang.

All leaped for it, but Mike won.

"Hello. Is that you, Cindy? (It's Cindy.) Where are you? What? Do you mean you can't tell me? Look here, young—What's that? 'Trust you'? You'd *better* be home in a few days. I don't like it. There's nothing we can do ... I have to tell Denny Slocum. Well, it's a mystery to me. Goodbye, honey."

The women said nothing, but their eyes pleaded for information.

"That was Cindy," Mike said redundantly. "I guess she's OK; so is Ben. They're together. Said something about being in danger, but they're OK right now. We'll just have to wait.

The women held each other, barely satisfied.

"Oh, by the way," said Mike, turning, "Cindy said to tell you that they didn't run away and get married!"

It was the week before the Newcastle Fair, and mighty were the preparations for the city's annual week-long celebration. Bunting and band uniforms were shaken out of winter's mothballs. Instruments were polished and cleaned. Telephones jangled, and the wires hummed as organizers took care of details. Mayor Morse and the city fathers sat in the air-conditioned Buggywhip Tavern, quaffing cold beers and talking about the old days. Floats from clubs and lodges were constructed and decorated, and horses were curried, groomed, and tricked out for the big days. Small boys wove crepe paper into the spokes of their bicycles. Colonel Jim Potter brushed his high-collared World War I uniform and dreamed of the Argonne, while VFW members and American Legionnaires whitened and polished their uniforms.

This was Newcastle's biggest parade, the Fourth. As it marched up Emporium Avenue to the fairgrounds, the gates ritualistically opening to welcome the marchers, Newcastle began a week wherein very little work was done, or even thought of.

Up on the fairgrounds, work crews labored on the half-mile oval track, preparing it for seven days of harness racing. The grandstand was newly painted, and the stage out front was hung with red, white, and blue bunting. Three big flags—the American, the Vermont, and the fair—were ironed and carefully folded for the ceremonial flag raising. These banners would fly over the fairgrounds all week.

The fairgrounds were dominated by a huge red, white, and blue grandstand, and spreading out from it were dozens of one-story buildings, housing sheep, goats, show and draft horses, seven kinds of dairy cattle and polled Hereford beef animals, pigs, a variety of hens, cocks and cockerels, rabbits, turkeys, dogs, puppies, cats and kittens, ponies and pony rides, wild game and fish. If it walked, jumped, ran, slithered, flew, or swam, it was there. The buildings also hosted early summer squash and baskets full of zucchini, peas, a huge display of seven varieties of lettuce, called the Salad Bowl. Pies, cakes, candies, breads, muffins, biscuits, jams and jellies, preserved peaches—if you could eat it, it was there. In fact, the fair in full swing resembled nothing more than a giant barnyard, a cacophony of moos, cluckings and squallings, all surrounded by the smells of popcorn and onion, and lit up by a dazzling

array of colored lights. Some of these lights were station-
ary; others whipped and turned, rose and fell, in glowing
dots or shimmering waterfalls.

Music drove everything and everybody along during
fair days and nights. In the morning dew, bright and cool,
with trotters thumping softly along the dusty dirt track, it
was patriotic airs. Often it was Dixieland jazz, which is
good daytime music. Later, trumpet blasts called the horses
to the starting gates, and, between races, the sounds of old-
time fiddling cut the dust of the last dash. And at night the
plaintive calls of country singers lay over the grandstand
like full clouds, sad but not raining yet:

> *Ah was married to one,*
> *Then another.*
> *They couldn't keep*
> *Me satisfied,*
> *So I drove off the one,*
> *Then t'other.*
> *And now Ah'm so sad*
> *I could die!*
>
> *Don't give me no weddin' rings,*
> *No preachers, no champagne 'n things,*
> *Cause Ah'm footloose and walkin',*
> *And Ah'm all done with talkin',*
> *Yore the queen, but Ah ain't no king!*

Ben and Cindy, like many of the high school kids in
Newcastle, had gotten jobs at the fair. The pay was mini-
mal, but the fringe benefits outweighed the meager salary,
for they got gate passes, which let the bearer in any gate at
any time.

William (Wild Bill) Shoulders was a jolly sort of man who every year brought two tractor-trailer loads of sound equipment to the Newcastle Fair from his headquarters in Lancaster, Pennsylvania. Then he and his harried assistant, running around in an electric golf cart, rigged the whole fairgrounds with sound systems and loudspeakers—a system so sensitive that if you opened a beer in the sound truck it could be heard in the main cattle arena ten acres away. Bill and his cohorts set themselves up comfortably behind the main stage (facing the grandstand), and busily brought the sounds of the fair to one and all.

On this opening day it was hot, delightfully skin tightening, scalp blistering hot. Bill was cooling some wine underneath the awning of his sound studio and living trailer. He had just opened an icy-cold diet soda when he noticed a blond kid hanging around, eyeing him.

"Hi ya, kid." Bill greeted him jovially. "Hot enough for ya?"

"Yeah, it's pretty hot." The kid kicked at the ground.

"Ever see anything like this?" said Bill as he waved grandly at his sound settlement. He was thinking that it was the same at every fair, carnival, rodeo, or show he had worked in his twenty years in the business. There was always some kid who wanted to know everything there was to know about electronics and sound systems. And to judge by the questions, they wanted to know it all in about fifteen minutes. This was the one in Newcastle. Bill had gotten so that he could spot them right away.

"No," the kid answered slowly, "I don't think I ever have."

Just then a great gray cat with yellow eyes slunk out from under the truck. Bill started and said, "That yer cat?

He's a beauty. My wife is the cat lover in our family." He paused. "Anyhoo, care to see how it works?"

"Gee, sure, I'd appreciate that," said the kid, and they went inside the air-conditioned trailer. The gray cat also slipped in unnoticed.

Inside there was an impressive array of dials and gauges, needles flickering, slide controls, microphones, and wires. The master control board faced three tinted plate-glass windows. Sitting properly, an announcer could view half the world from this vantage, and describe it to the other half. But Bill noticed the kid was more interested in the tape unit. "What do you think of that rig?"

"It sure doesn't look like any tape recorder I've ever seen."

"Or likely to, 'cause it ain't like any other machine. I designed and built that one myself. Here, lemme show you."

Bill was proud of this system. He had offered it to Sony and some of the other manufacturers, but they turned it down as not suitable for the mass markets they sold to.

"First of all, it can take any kind of recording tape, disk, cartridge, or cassette *instantly*. All you do is push this control to whatever kind it is, drop your recording in here, and push this button. Then you're on."

"No threading or fooling with recording heads?" asked his visitor.

"Nope," said Bill realizing the kid knew something about it. "Y'see, it's all done with magnetism and a small laser. Fully automatic, to use an old-fashioned term."

"Wow!"

"And that's not all. You can play two kinds of recordings on this at the same time."

"I don't get it."

"Supposing you have someone talking on one tape, and some music on a cassette, and you wanted to pipe them out together. Just turn this, insert in there, and press that one. And you have a whole production. I'm working on one that will take three simultaneous recordings." Bill took a big drink of his soda. He loved showing his electronic marvels. "One more thing: if someone is talking or singing on the microphones on the main stage, you can give them all kinds of background music and sound."

"I gotta go now, Mister," said the boy. "Thanks."

Bill was also used to these abrupt departures. Maybe it was more than they could handle in one day, he thought.

"OK, champ."

"And thanks for showing me."

"Anytime, anytime at all." Bill went back to cooling his wine.

Ben and Cindy fidgeted at one corner of the long, gold-colored building that housed all the arts and crafts shown at the fair. "You don't suppose he got caught?" asked Cindy.

"Naw, what's to catch? All he's doing is finding out how the system works. Didn't Beechmont say that the sound guy had been coming to the fair for years and liked to show off his fancy equipment?" asked Ben. He sounded confident.

"I suppose you're right. Wait, here he comes now," Cindy said.

A diminutive figure walked slowly across the oval's grassy infield toward the low guardrails, slowly, almost drifting.

"Cripes, I wish he'd hurry up," Cindy said.

Ben muttered, "Move it, you little twerp, or it's head-pounding time."

Finally, Pete O'Rourke dragged himself over to Ben and Cindy.

"Gee, you got lead weights stuck in your pants? Talk about Joe Slow," said Ben.

Cindy glared at her little brother. "Did you learn how it's done?"

But Pete looked dazed, staring back unfocused at the sound trucks. "Wow," he breathed.

By this time Ben was beside himself. "What now? Speak up, or I'll give you something to put you to sleep permanently!"

"Oh, wow," Pete sighed.

"Listen, you," Ben started.

But Cindy stopped him. "Let me handle this. Peter, dear, did you like the sound trucks? Why not tell us about them." Cindy smiled sweetly through clenched teeth.

The young genius began to rise to the surface. "Wow, you should see it. That guy has gear they haven't even thought of. That's what I'm going to be—a sound man. I think I'll run away from home."

"You can run away from home after you do what you promised. Did you learn how to set it up?" demanded Cindy.

"What? Oh yeah, simple. There's nothing to it."

"OK then, here's the tape recording. We told you when we want it played."

"Yeah, I gotcha, but I wish someone would tell me what was going on," Pete said, his voice getting shrill. He was coming back to his usual self.

"Peter-r-r." Cindy's voice took on a warning edge.

"OK, OK."

Ben said in his most ominous Dr. Fu Manchu voice, "*If you fail in this mission, do not bother to return.*"

"Rats," said Pete under his breath. He grabbed the tape and took off.

"We'd better go over our parts," Cindy said, pushing her big glasses up on her nose. "Now, Beechmont said he would be in the grandstand for the ceremonies. And he said we should be around, too."

"Sounds good, but what about Nick?" asked Ben.

"You remember, Nick said he had something to do, something important."

"Boy, I don't know, we're takin' some awful chances. Anybody seen that lawyer?" asked Ben.

"He's still wandering around town. I heard they won't even let him march in the parade, he's gotten so weird." Cindy looked at Ben. "Hey, don't be so worried. Everything's going to be all right."

"Gees, I hope so." Ben thought a minute and said, "Sure, it's going to be OK."

Far away, under this clear, hot, and almost cloudless sky, the Fourth of July Parade began forming into sections, and a slight breeze carried the sound of the brass bands tuning up. A little kid came roaring up to the main gate of the fairground, pumping furiously on his gaily bedecked bike, and shouted, "They're comin', they're comin'!" And fair officials—farmers, and dairymen, resplendent in unaccustomed suits, neckties, and green and yellow chest sashes—looked beyond and down Main Street to behold the great Newcastle Independence Day parade.

Marching, sometimes ten abreast, flags and pennants waving and dipping in rhythm, brass instruments glinting in the sun, special cars and floats moving and stopping, horses neighing and cantering, the parade was not unlike triumphal Roman legions glorying in conquest as they approached the Imperial City.

Right up front were the mayor and city fathers. The aldermen still looked as if they could use massive doses of antacids, but the mayor was smiling broadly, having heeded the advice of his doctor in the last few weeks and cut out the cigars and chocolate. Anyway, he loved parades and all the official pomp—it made him feel like a general. And it was a beautiful day.

Behind them, the American Legion band engaged in martial airs and popular tunes of the day. The band was in turn followed by flower and crepe paper festooned floats representing civic groups. One notorious saloon (not Pica's Grill) had managed to sneak a float into the parade under the guise of the "Imperial Bibulous Marching and Benevolent Society." This raucous crew, lurching as they went by, toasted the watchers. Crowds of Boy Scouts, Girl Scouts, Brownies, Cub Scouts, Little Leaguers, and a hundred mothers walked in a vague sense of order, determined and proud. And everywhere kids on decorated bikes darted like waterbugs.

Having reached the gates, the front line of marchers halted, causing a ripple to travel back through the ranks, finally reaching a tiny Cub Scout, who whispered to his Den Mother that he "had to go potty."

The mayor, grasping a long-bladed pair of shears, intoned, "In my capacity as mayor of the city of Newcastle, I hereby declare the fairgrounds open." With that he snipped the long green ribbon, and the fair was offically open.

The parade and the ribbon cutting were part of a tradition that stretched back to the mid-nineteenth century when the fair first moved into the city from the rural wilderness that was Newcastle County.

With the ceremony completed, people began to flood onto the grounds. These grounds, which minutes before lay silent and shiny under the sun, now began to move and pulse with life. And the first movement was that of the carnival rides. Slowly they cranked into action—the great round wheels, the swinging seats, the long arms and tortuous turns of track, the loud rock music, and the bearded and disheveled ride attendants, all beckoning, waving, and enticing as families and kids took their first tentative steps into the carnival.

A growly, metallic, magnified voice said, "I-10, B-17, O-47. We have a bingo. Hold all cards."

The heavenly smell of frying foods—onions, sausage, hamburgers and hot dogs, bread dough, potatoes, and peppers—spread like a junk food junkie's dream. Clouds of cotton candy and maple floss, captured on paper cones in tiny hands, floated through the crowds.

"Three balls for a dime. Everybody's a winner. Three balls for a dime." Sturdy farm boys surveyed the carnival hanky-panks warily as open-shirted carnies and tight-bloused girls practiced their art of seduction. The rubes versus the carnies, and who will win?

But it was, after all, the glorious Fourth and time for politicians, so the many marchers headed for the huge grandstand where the Newcastle City Band was busily playing the "King Cotton March." On the stage, at least two dozen chairs waited patiently, ready to receive the rear ends of all the dignitaries. This was Newcastle's big political speechifying day of the year. It was a time when politicos of every stripe managed to sit together in uneasy harmony under the broiling July sun, and woo the citizenry in a perfect halo of patriotism.

Greeting the mayor was Vermont's senior senator, a tall, silver-haired man of impeccable stature. Beside him, smiling, was the state's lone congressman, a bright young lawyer whose antecedents came up from Connecticut to settle the hard land of Vermont in 1799. Activity eddied the crowd at the grandstand entrance as, sirens wailing, the big black limousine of the governor drew up. Out stepped this worthy, a big man with a small head of curly hair, his suit-jacket buttoned tightly around what old-timers called his "corporation."

The grandstand filled up. Kids in white caps hawked cold soda, ice cream, popcorn, and fair programs. The band played away: the tuba player noticed that drops of his perspiration sizzled as they fell on the bright metal of his instrument.

The stage was set as the president of Newcastle Fair stepped up to the microphone and opened his mouth.

"Gino, siddown and shut up!" boomed forth from loud-speakers all over the fairgrounds. It was not the anticipated warm words of welcome from the fair president, but unmistakably: "Gino, siddown and shut up!" It was the mayor's voice, and a tribute to Wild Bill Shoulder's electronic art.

An awful silence filled the grandstand. Then the loud-speakers bellowed forth with a lot of voices talking at once, then a pause. Then a single, spooky voice, clear and easily understood, began to talk. People in the grandstand, who had turned to one another in amazement, were now saying, "Sshh-ssh, listen. Listen to it."

They listened as the voice told of a royal grant, of the city not being what it was supposed to be. They really listened.

Meanwhile, Wild Bill had been monitoring the stage at his control box in the stands. Suddenly realizing he was not hearing what he supposed he should be hearing, he tore off his earphones and raced down the grandstand. Up-setting a small boy, whose cups and Cokes flew all over the seats, Bill sprinted across the track to his trailer. Tearing open the sliding glass door, he recoiled.

The tape recorder was on, slowly running a cassette, but he couldn't turn it off for the entire machine was over-run by cats. Yellow cats, tiger cats, black cats, white cats, crawled, curled, snarled, and hissed. This feline phalanx seemed to be dominated by a great, gray cat with golden eyes.

Just then there was a roar from the grandstand crowd. Dashing outside, Bill saw that everyone was now gazing skyward. Naturally, he looked up. High in the blue sky, tiny and black, a biplane swooped and turned, jets of pure white vapor spouting from its belly. It was a skywriter, and several letters were already standing out boldly against the blue:

M A

Like the rest of the crowd, Wild Bill watched.

M A Y O

He was also aware that the voices over the loudspeaker continued, sometimes shouting, often silent except for that cold, harrowing voice talking about royal grants and murder.

M A Y O R

Cindy, who was sitting near the track gate, yelled in the hubbub to Ben, "That's got to be Nick. But where is Beechmont?"

M A Y O R   T E

The airplane dipped and swirled, puffing out the giant letters with ease.

MAYOR TELL

Gordy Morse, when he heard his own voice boom over the loudspeaker, felt his good feeling slip away. And as the broadcast went on he soon realized that it was a recording of the secret executive council meeting. Galvanized into action, he began waving his arms, "Shoot that plane down! Call out the National Guard. Call out the jets."

MAYOR TELL TRU

The governor hastily whispered to his state police aides, "Get me the hell out of here!" Then, realizing that the crowd might notice his retreat, he said, "No, never mind. Have to stand fast."

MAYOR TELL TRUTH

As if it had been carefully staged, the last bit of skywriting coincided with John Arnold's eerie voice cutting through the crowd's murmur: "Newcastle is not legal!"

And again that silence, followed by some kid's voice shouting, "Look at the plane!"

The skywriter, having finished his chore, brought his plane down into a beautiful three-point landing on the track. He hopped lightly from the plane, wearing a pure white flying jumper, an old-fashioned leather helmet, and goggles. He gripped a brass-filligreed, long black box. And he grinned.

Cindy had guessed right—it was Nick Tomasi, and boy, did he look great. Cindy later recalled that she had never seen Nick so relaxed, with such a nice smile. Ben said he looked like the hero in an old flying movie. The crowd cheered and applauded, and the bandmaster, taking this as a cue, tapped his baton, and the Newcastle City Band broke into "El Capitan."

Nick started to mount the small stairway to the stage, but two burly state troopers barred his way.

"They're going to stop him. Oh Ben, what can we do?" asked Cindy.

She looked around wildly and spotted her father and mother, just entering the grandstand. Scrambling to her father she panted, "Dad, oh Dad, you've got to help him. Please, it's important, for the whole town. It's what Ben and I have been working on in our history project."

"Hold on. What are ya talking about?" he said.

"Please Dad, no time to explain. Please help!"

Michael O'Rourke looked into his daughter's eyes, and there was something there that caused him to move swiftly. He lifted his head and bawled, "Brawlers, Brawlers, *Iron Man Down.*" It was his old gang's secret call when a member needed help.

With that, middle-aged men all over the grandstand jumped up—fat men, bald men, thin men, men barely able to totter and run, stumbled or staggered to the rallying voice. The formed a protective phalanx around Mike, and he led them in a swarm across the track.

Nick, struggling with troopers and politicians, was about to square off, and already had his fists clenched when this motley collection of ex-street brawlers swept his opposition away. A path began to open up to the microphone. Mike bumped up against someone busily shoving bodies aside, turned, and saw Chief Dennis Slocum in full dress uniform.

"Denny, what'n hell is the law doin' here?"

"Hell, Mike, I was a Brawler before I was a cop!"

And they both went happily back to work. For a moment the state troopers resisted, but tactics learned on the streets of Newcastle paid off. One trooper reached for his pistol, a huge, ugly magnum, but another, looking at him with disgust, said, "Put that damn thing away!"

The politicians, caught between two struggling masses, were horrified as they saw their dignity slipping away. The Washington senator said, "Look at them, they're actually enjoying all this!"

The crowd, swelled by people who had heard about the ruckus on the grandstand, cheered lustily. The bandmaster, still thinking this was all part of the show, waved his perspiring musicians into "Liberty Bell."

The mayor (another old South Street Brawler) bullied his way to Nick. "C'mon boy, grab ahold of my belt and hang on!" With that, he lowered his head and worked his short, powerful body like the guard he once was on the Newcastle High football team as the two men bashed their way the last few yards to the microphone. Politicians and state troopers flew in all directions. The crowd gave a mighty roar.

Then suddenly all was silent. A flute tootled its last note, and a hush fell over the crowd as the hot sun blazed relentlessly. Nick stepped smartly up to the microphone, still holding the long, black box.

He spoke, and his deep, rich voice filled the fairgrounds. "Citizens of Newcastle, you all know me!"

He paused as voices from the crowd spoke up. "Sure do, Nick."

"That's Nick Tomasi, remember him?"

"Best damn halfback St. Francis ever had."

Nick raised his hands for silence and said, "Do you know what's going on here?"

"NO!" yelled the crowd.

"OK, there's a reason for my skywriting, for that tape recording you just heard, and for what's in this black box. Now, I'm going to call on the mayor to tell us about it. C'mon, Mayor."

Newcastle's chief citizen, still feeling exhilarated by his brief return to football glory, suddenly had an intense desire for a cigar and an almond chocolate bar. He felt thousands of eyes upon him. Well, his had been a nice political career while it lasted. He cleared his throat and launched into his speech: "People of Newcastle, the point of all this—why Nick wrote up in the sky for me to tell the truth—is that the city of Newcastle doesn't belong to us!"

There was a stunned silence, then whispers, murmurs growing into shouts: "What's he mean?"

"What doesn't belong to us?"

"Hell, I'm a taxpayer!"

"Explain yourself, Gordy!"

"OK, OK, I'm tryin'," said Mayor Morse as he wiped his dripping brow. "It seems that a long time ago, one of our founders murdered the man that actually owned all the ground upon which sits Newcastle. That guy got it direct from the king of England. The federal government, since the time of George Washington, has upheld all these royal land grants, which means that if there is a direct descendant, that person owns Newcastle."

And a long gasp came from the crowd.

"Now listen to me. A lawyer here in town, a direct descendant of the guy who did the murdering, brought this information to me and the city council," Morse said. Wiping his face again with a soaked handkerchief, Gordon Morse took a last look at his political career sinking out of sight, and plunged on. "We, the city council and I, decided to have the documents proving all this burned, and, I'm ashamed to say, not tell you people about it." He hesitated, then concluded, "I was wrong."

He waited for the storm of abuse. Instead, a mighty cheer broke out. "Atta boy, Gordy!"

"Tell it like it is!"

"Three cheers for Mayor Morse!"

The crowd broke into huzzahs. The mayor was stupified, but was shrewd enough to see his political career start rising again like a smiling sun on the horizon.

Nick gained the microphone again and said, "Luckily, all the documents are safe, here in this box. They weren't burned."

The crowd became restive, talking among themselves. Someone shouted, "What do we do?"

The mayor (now dreaming up a campaign as Honest Gordy—He's Not Afraid to Say He's Wrong) said, "I don't know. We'll have to get the state in on this. However, if there is an heir of Jeffrey Walker out there among you people, maybe he or she could let us know."

Nick grabbed the microphone and said, "There is an heir, and he's right here. And there's two Newcastle High kids that really were the ones who discovered the whole thing. I'm going to ask Beechmont Walker and Cindy O'Rourke and Ben Weisman to come up here."

Ben and Cindy, as they stood up automatically, craned to find Beechmont. They looked up and down the grandstand and along the long row of chairs stretching to the sides of them. No Beechmont. And Nick was urging them across the track to the stage.

Cindy turned to Ben, "Oh, where is he?"

And a quiet voice behind her said, "Someone lookin' for me?"

"Beeeechmont!" she cried, and flung herself into his arms.

Ben tugged at her arm. "C'mon, they want us up there."

So the three walked across the track and scampered up on the stage, past the shocked faces of the politicians, the state police, and the South Street Brawlers, right to center stage. Cindy thought she hadn't seen so many people in all her life.

"Ladies and gentlemen, this is Beechmont Turner Walker, the direct descendant of Captain Jack Turner, the true founder of Newcastle!"

There was loud applause from the crowd.

"And these two, Cindy and Ben, are the ones we can thank for having guts enough to stick with it and uncover the true story."

More cheers and applause from the crowd. Beechmont put his arms around Ben and Cindy and they stood there with the whole town cheering them. And up in the stands, Cindy's and Ben's history teacher, Mr. Rafshoon, totally lost his usual aloof and sarcastic manner and commenced whacking the man next to him on the back, yelling, "They're my kids. They're in my class! How about that? Why, they're my best students!" The bandmaster, wanting to join in the accolade, swung his baton, and the Newcastle City Band burst into "American Patrol."

Wild Bill Shoulders, while watching these events, suddenly thought of his beloved sound trailer. He ran back and found it quiet. Not a trace of cats. The tape recorder was turned off, and the tape was gone.

John Arnold had been in the crowd. He had watched and heard the heroics and cheering. He had sneered at that mealy-mouthed bastard, Gordy Morse, and glared with a transcendent malevolence at Beechmont as he mounted the stage. And he knew that he was defeated. He was tired and he wanted no more of Newcastle. He would leave and he would not return. A great weakness came over him as he turned his back on the gathered citizens of Newcastle and made his way through the fairgoers jamming the midway, laughing and clacking.

"Idiots!" he said bitterly, and he had a sinking sensation. He gasped for air, struggling toward the gate at the far end of the grounds where he got into his car and sat, panting.

"Oh God, oh God, oh God, get me out of here," he moaned. He felt his face, and despite the ninety-degree day, it was clammy and cold.

Starting the car, he headed south, down the valley highway and away from the historic ground where once, long ago, two men struggled and one man died.

PHOTO BY DON WICKMAN

Peter Cooper lives in Rutland, Vermont, where he is director of substance-abuse treatment agency. "I've always been a writer," he points out, but over the years he's also found time to be a Western Union boy, soda jerk, boat painter, tree surgeon, bartender, Associated Press caption writer, trade magazine editor, newspaper publisher, and publicity director for the Vermont State Fair. He is also active in Little Theatre productions and describes himself as "a frustrated musician." The Secret Papers of Julia Templeton is his first book.